No Small Thing

Natale Ghent

CANDLEWICK PRESS
CAMBRIDGE, MASSACHUSETTS

First published by HarperCollins Canada, 2003
Copyright © 2003 by Natale Ghent

First U.S. edition 2005

This paperback edition was specially produced for Scholastic Book
Fairs (2005) by arrangement with Candlewick Press, Inc., and is only
available for distribution through the school market.

Library of Congress Cataloging-in-Publication Data is available.

Library of Congress Catalog Card Number 2003065281

ISBN 0-7636-2861-1 (Scholastic edition)

2   4   6   8   10   9   7   5   3   1

Printed in the United States of America

This book was typeset in Sabon.

Candlewick Press
2067 Massachusetts Avenue
Cambridge, Massachusetts 02140

visit us at www.candlewick.com

To Wesley and Brian,
who are never too tired for the ride

how it all starts

Sometimes, something as small as an ad in the daily newspaper can change your whole life. That's what happened to Cid, Queenie, and me one summer. It was 1977, the year of broken things. *Star Wars* opened and broke the record at the Eastview Theater by running for thirteen weeks in a row. Queenie broke her collarbone. And Cheryl Hanson broke my heart. This is how the ad read:

PONY TO GIVE AWAY TO GOOD HOME.
CALL BEFORE 4 P.M.

"Oh, my gosh, call it!" Cid says, grabbing at the newspaper in my hand.

I jerk the paper away and hold it over my head. "Why do I always have to do all the calling?" I ask her. "You're the oldest. Why don't you call, for once?" I say this just to bug her. I know that I'll be the one to call because I'm a boy and I'm not afraid of anything.

Cid is the oldest, but you wouldn't know it half the time. If she's not bossing you around, she's acting like a baby. She'll never call about the ad because she hates talking to people, even if it's for something as good as a pony for free. I don't mind talking. I like to read, too, which is odd for a boy. I like words and the way they sound. I guess that's why I skipped a grade in school. It's not like I go around showing off or anything. That would be the fastest way to get myself beat up. But it gives you power to know words, Ma says. And I can use all the power I can get, because, let me tell you, being a boy with two sisters isn't easy. Especially a sister like Cid.

Now, Queenie, she isn't like most girls. She's as good as a little brother, really. She never squeals on me or makes a big deal when she's hurt or tries to boss anyone. Some people think she's different because of the way she goes off in her own world sometimes. It doesn't mean she's crazy. It's just her way of dealing with things, I guess. Anyway, Ma says I cried when Queenie came out a girl because I wanted a brother so badly. But that was a long time ago. . . .

"You're better at talking than me, Nat," Cid says in a whine. "You've got a paper route and you're used to talking to people."

She called me Nat. I know she doesn't mean it. My name is Nathaniel, and people who like me call me Nat. Ma calls me Nat and Queenie calls me Nat, but Cid almost never does because we fight so much. She's just doing it to get what she wants, but it won't work. She lunges for the paper again. I move it easily behind my back and around to the side, just to irritate her.

"If you're not going to call, then let me do it!" she yells, grabbing my sweatshirt at the neck and twisting it into a knot with her fist. Her short brown hair falls out from behind her ears. Her bottom lip is quivering, and her hazel eyes are burning like hot coals— but I don't care. I'm not afraid of her, even though she's fourteen. I can get the better of her, and I'm only twelve. Queenie is eight.

"You think you can solve everything like that," I say in the calm, cool voice that she hates.

She pulls her arm back like she's really going to

punch me, but she won't do it—not with Ma so close in the next room.

"Ma! Nathaniel won't give me the newspaper!" she yells, as though Ma would care. Ma doesn't answer. I cock one eyebrow just to show Cid that I'm not worried at all. Her face screws up and her eyes turn all black, and I know I've made her really furious.

Just then, Queenie comes bursting into the kitchen through the mudroom door. Her face glistens with tiny beads of sweat. I can tell she's been running. Her long gold hair hangs in two fuzzy braids down her back. She pulls off her worn yellow windbreaker, then kicks off her sneakers. They land against the mudroom door with two loud thumps.

"Stop that thumping!" Ma yells from her little bedroom off the kitchen.

I give Queenie the look, and then I unfold the newspaper in the important way I'd seen Dad do when we all used to live together. "Someone's giving a pony away for free."

Queenie's face lights up—just like I knew it would. She runs across the kitchen to look at the paper.

"Look. It's right here: 'Pony to give away to good home.'" I trace the words with my finger so she can

4

follow them, even though I know she can read as well as I can.

"Is it true?" she asks in her small voice, her green eyes all wide like the kids you see in toy commercials on the TV. Just like that. Only Queenie is the real deal—"the genuine article," as Dad used to say. Those kids on the TV, they're just acting. You know once the camera stops rolling, they're screaming for things and yelling at their parents and stuff. But not Queenie. Everybody loves her. Even strangers on the street. Because she's sweet inside and out, and everyone can see that. I even convinced her once that spaghetti grows on trees.

"Course it's true," I say. "It's in the paper, isn't it?"

"What color do you think he is, Nat?" she asks, holding on to my sleeve. "Do you think he's broke to ride? Maybe someone's taken him already. Maybe he's already gone and we're just getting our hopes up for nothing."

Her words come out in a rush, and she doesn't even take a breath between sentences.

"I haven't called to find out yet. Cid's been bugging me, so I haven't had a chance."

Cid shoots me a look full of hate.

"Maybe he's already gone," Queenie says again, wistfully.

"Why don't you just call the number instead of torturing us?" Cid snaps at me.

I ignore her and turn to Queenie. "I'm going to call about the pony right now, but you have to promise me something. You have to promise not to tell Ma, do you hear me? She'll just say no and talk about how we can't afford it and everything."

Queenie makes a motion to button her lips and crosses her heart with her finger.

We move into the hallway and I pick up the phone. "Read the number out to me," I say, handing Queenie the paper. She reads the number out and I dial. The phone rings three times before someone picks it up. It's a woman with a beautiful, light voice like the women in the black-and-white movies Ma sometimes watches at night.

"I'm calling about the pony," I say.

"Yes."

"Do you still have it?"

"Yes."

I nod my head excitedly at Queenie, who grabs my sleeve.

"Would you like to come and see him?" the woman asks.

"Oh, yes," I say, because now I'm getting hopeful, too. It may seem funny for a boy to get hopeful about something like a pony, and I can't explain it, really. I suppose I'm doing it for Queenie more than anyone, and people will just have to accept that explanation. But all the same, I'm hopeful.

The woman gives me directions to her farm. I repeat them to Cid, who scribbles them with a pencil on the back of the phone book. I'm a better writer than she is, but I don't want to listen to the woman and write at the same time. Besides, Cid has to do something to help, even if she doesn't like to talk to people.

"Ma'am," I say softly when she's finished with the directions, "will you promise not to give him away until we have a chance to see him? We can't come until this afternoon, so will you promise to keep him until then?" There is a terrible silence, and I know that she is thinking about what she should do. But then she promises at last and asks for my name, and I give it to her. Nathaniel Howard Estabrooks. I thank the woman and hang up the phone.

"She's going to hold him for us."

Queenie throws her arms around me. I untangle her and look into her face.

"Don't tell Ma where we're going," I tell her. "It'll be OK. She'll just think we've gone to the park like we always do."

Queenie nods, then hurries into the mudroom to grab her sneakers. Cid follows her. I tear off the piece of phone book with the directions and cram it into the back pocket of my jeans, then sneak upstairs to get my money. The pony may be free, but we're going to have to pay to rent a stall and get him a few other things he may need—like hay, and a halter if he doesn't have one already.

I keep my money hidden in a cigar box behind the dresser in my bedroom. Dad gave me the box, but that's not why I use it. I just don't have anything better. I reach behind the dresser and pull out the box. White Owl cigars. His favorite. I sniff the box before I open it. It still smells earthy and kind of sweet from the tobacco.

I open it and grab the wad of money from inside. It's rolled in a bundle and held together with a green rubber band. I count it, just to be sure it's all there, and it is: ninety-five dollars and thirty-six cents. I managed to save it from my paper route. It took me almost a year. I'd never tell anyone I have it, not even Queenie. It's not that I'm selfish or anything. I just think it's best to keep quiet about it. I did try to give some to Ma once. She wouldn't have it. She told me it was mine and that I'd earned it. I know she could have used it to help out with groceries and things, but pride wouldn't let her take money from her own son. It made me feel good to be able to offer it to her. But secretly, I'm glad she let me keep it.

I roll the money back up, secure it with the rubber band, then push it into my pocket. When I go downstairs, I find Cid and Queenie sitting on the back stoop. Queenie sees me and starts talking all in a rush again.

"I can't believe the pony is still there. She said he's beautiful, right? I wonder what color he is. How come no other kids got him? Why is she giving him away? Maybe he's meant to be ours. . . . And how are we going to get out there to see him, because Ma sure won't give us money for a taxi?"

With this last question, Queenie and Cid both look at me. I turn away like I'm thinking, even though I already know the answer.

"We're going to walk," I finally say in the matter-of-fact way Ma does when she tells us there's no milk in the house and there won't be any tomorrow, either. She says it like this so we'll be strong about it and not complain.

"Walk?" Cid moans. "It's way out past the Tenth Line! We won't get there until next week."

"Not if it's up to you," I scoff. "Get your shoes on and let's go."

Cid rolls her eyes and sighs. She knows I hate when she does this.

"You can come along with us and have fun or you can stay here and stew."

I know this will shut Cid up, and it does. She stuffs her feet angrily into her shoes.

"We'll have to get the pony some hay and oats," Queenie says, pulling her sneakers over her floppy socks. Her socks are always floppy.

"Fix your socks or you'll get a blister," I tell her. "We'll get him everything he needs."

"With what money?" Cid demands. "And how are we supposed to get him home?"

I ignore her question, tying my shoes very carefully with a double knot, because I know we have a long way to go—way out past the Tenth Line and then some. I smooth my hair to one side and pull up my own socks. Queenie is waiting patiently for an answer, but Cid is ready to smack me.

"We're going to ride him home."

the long journey

It takes about an hour just to walk to where the trees start to unfold and the road turns to gravel at the edge of town. I know Queenie has a blister already from her socks, which are always too big. Yet, even though she's little, she won't complain, because out of the three of us, she wants the pony most of all. I don't know why this is, really. She's too young to remember much about the life we used to have.

We used to live in a beautiful house on the outskirts of town with two ponies and some ducks and chickens, too. Then Dad left and things changed. We sold the house and the ponies and all their tack and everything. Ma made us. It's like she tried to erase her life with Dad completely, and erased all our lives in the process. But a life with ponies doesn't erase easily. It stays inside you and burns in your heart like a little gas flame.

Maybe Queenie just wants a chance at "the good old days." That's what Dad used to call it when he would tell us about earlier times. Maybe it's my fault for making our old life sound so wonderful, like Cid and I had all the fun. Queenie probably just wants a chance at what Cid and I already had. Living in town would be totally horrible except for the fact that Eastview isn't very big. Only twenty-seven thousand people. You can walk past the buildings and houses in no time and be in the country pretty easily.

I look over at Queenie. She's holding the bridle she got for her birthday two years ago, the reins gently slapping against her thigh as she walks and hums "Hush Little Baby."

Ma was so confused about the bridle. "You haven't even got a horse to ride," she said. "And besides, we live in town now, in case you kids haven't noticed."

But Queenie didn't care where we lived. She wanted that bridle and didn't want anything else, she said. Ma just sighed. I don't know where she found the money. The snaffle bit alone must have cost twenty-five dollars.

Cid says the man at the co-op is secretly in love with Ma and gave her a good deal. But he's wasting his time, if you ask me. Ma hasn't seen a man since Dad left us four years ago.

I remember the day he drove away, his face smiling through the window of his silver Pontiac Parisienne. I have a picture of him and me in that car. I keep it in the drawer of my night table. I was only eight the day he left, but somehow I knew he was never coming back. Ma won't talk about it. Cid says she hates him. Queenie was too young to remember much. Sometimes I think I see him around, driving down the highway in that car, or ducking through an alley, or at the corner store—but it's never him. It's just wishful thinking, or memories playing tricks on me like ghosts, or something. I've never told anyone about this, not even Ma.

Anyway, Queenie slept with that bridle in her bed for months after she got it, like she was expecting a pony to trot right out of her dreams and into her bedroom. Now she keeps it on a hook by her bed, because Ma insisted. Queenie takes it down from the hook once a week to clean it and oil the leather. Ma must think it's foolishness, but she would never say a word because she loves Queenie so dearly. I'm sure she wishes she had the money to buy Queenie a pony to go with the bridle. But that will never happen. Not the way we live.

There isn't enough food on the table half the time. Not that Ma isn't trying. She has her job as a legal secretary at this dingy office next to Woolworth's. It's just that it isn't easy for a woman on her own to take care of three kids. I try to be strong, to set an example for Queenie and Cid, but sometimes I wish we were more like other people, with their cars and nice homes and things.

We've been walking for nearly two hours now. Our little town is lost from sight. The gravel road unwinds like a dusty ribbon in front of us. There is the smell of green in the air, and the sunlight winks at us through the trees.

Queenie has a funny little dance in her walk sometimes. She lurches forward, then throws her head back. She moves her fingers like she's sowing millions of tiny seeds all over the ground. That's what she does when she's thinking deep thoughts or when she wants to hide from the world. Ma says Queenie's thoughts just get all tangled up and she forgets where she is. I know she feels safe in the secret place inside her head, and that's why she goes there. She won't tell you what she's thinking about when she dances, so it's no good to ask. I bet she's thinking about the pony now. Dad never liked it when she danced in public. He said people will think she's "deficient" or something. But that's just nonsense, Ma says, even though I'm sure she worries about it, too. I let Queenie dance for a while before I grab her hand and run with her up the road for a bit.

Queenie isn't dancing anymore, and now we're all thinking and talking about the pony. We have so many questions. What color is he? How big? How old? Is he shod or barefoot? Cid and I start to fight over who gets to ride him first. Queenie says she'll think of a number and we can both take a guess and the closest one gets to ride first. I guess three, and Queenie says that's right. Cid fumes. She frowns at Queenie.

"You just said that so Nathaniel would win. How do I know the number was really three?"

Queenie doesn't answer but just keeps walking, a little smile on her face.

"See! She's lying!" Cid shouts. "It's not fair! This is such crap!"

Queenie and I keep walking along. I want to make Cid suffer for a while before I tell her that she can ride first, after all. I knew all along that I would let her ride the pony first. I just don't like her bossing me around all the time.

Eventually, we come to a fork in the road. I have to stop to figure out where we are. I squint at the trees and the sun. Beyond the trees, fields of green corn roll out to meet the blue sky. There's a little stone farmhouse perched on a hill at the end of a long lane. Nothing looks familiar. I don't know where to go.

"We're lost!" Cid says furiously.

"We are not lost!" I yell back, although I'm not sure. "Just keep your mouth shut or you'll scare Queenie!"

But Queenie doesn't look scared. I pull out the piece of phone book with the directions that Cid wrote. "The lady said we need to go left at this point," I say, trying to sound confident.

"You have no idea," Cid says, sneering.

"Then why don't you go your way and Queenie and I will go my way?"

Cid glowers at me. She doesn't have the guts to go off on her own.

We walk along in silence now, and it seems to be taking forever. I'm thinking that maybe I was wrong, and wouldn't Cid just love that. But the farm finally comes into sight. I know it's the right one because it has a small red barn with hay up to the rafters, just like the woman described over the phone. The house is bright yellow and as neat as a daffodil. There is a clean white picket fence around the perimeter. It looks like it would be more comfortable in the city. In fact, it looks as out of place here in the country as Dorothy's house looked after it dropped out of the sky in the land of Oz. There is a split-rail paddock to the right. A boy and a girl are sitting side by side on the top rail. They are as clean and orderly as the picket fence. They look as though they never fight. The boy is holding a Luke Skywalker action figure—the same one I want—twelve inches tall with the Tatooine desert outfit, grappling hook, and lightsaber. Removable tunic, pants, and boots. Fully articulated at the shoulders, legs, and hips. The stores have been sold out for weeks. I can't help but feel jealous. I bet he's lost all the accessories already. For a second I consider taking it from the kid.

And then I see the pony. He's standing in the middle of the paddock, sniffing the air. He is a pure white stallion with a black muzzle. His mane and tail are long and flowing. His eyes are dark and his coat is shaggy. He has three black hooves and one white one at the front. He's wearing a worn red webbing halter. And he is the most beautiful thing I have ever seen.

Queenie starts to run toward the paddock. Suddenly, I can't help myself and I start to run, too. Then all three of us are running. The boy yells to his mother that we're here. I don't even tell them my name as I skid up to the fence. I can't take my eyes off the pony. The mother comes out of the daffodil house, the screen door slapping shut behind her.

"Hello," she says cheerfully.

She has smooth blond hair and bright blue eyes. Her hands are delicate and soft, not at all like the farm wives I know. She's perfect in every way. She looks like a movie star.

"There he is," she says, pointing at the pony.

"He's beautiful," I say at last. "We'd like to take him."

"Don't you want to get a closer look?"

I shake my head.

Queenie is staring at the pony, not saying a thing. I know she's getting thoughtful.

"Don't your kids like to ride him?" she asks in a soft, faraway voice.

"Oh, they're kind of afraid of him," the woman admits. "He's a little bit wild. We only bought him because we thought the children would like a pony. But they never really took to him. Better to give him away to someone who will pay more attention to him."

"He's green," I say knowingly.

The woman looks at me. She smiles, brushing a lock of silky blond hair from her eyes. "Yes, I suppose that's what you call it."

I guess I'm showing off a bit here, but I can't help it. Like I said before, we didn't always live in town. We used to live in a big yellow house nicer than the daffodil. We practically grew up on horseback. "What's his name?" I ask.

"Smokey."

"Smokey." Queenie repeats the name in a whisper.

"He was all black when he was little," the woman explains. "It seems kind of funny to call him that, now that he's all white."

"I like it," Queenie says.

"Do you have a place to keep him?" the woman asks.

Queenie looks at me. Cid stares at the ground. I look the woman in the face and do something I know is wrong. I lie. "Yes, ma'am, we do."

I know it's not right to lie. Ma would be so disappointed if she knew. But I just can't go home without that pony. Not now. Not after coming all this way. I can't do that to Queenie.

Cid doesn't even protest like she normally would. That's because she knows I have to lie in this case. And then the lie gets bigger. I tell the woman that our mom would have come with us but she was busy working. She gave us permission to go ahead and get the pony ourselves. I tell her we would have borrowed a trailer from one of our friends, but they were all busy, too. I say that we are just going to walk him home and that will be all right because it isn't that far, really.

The woman looks at me kind of funny, but she doesn't question me.

"You can keep the halter. We have a lead to match and some brushes. You can take those, too." She disappears into the barn, then reappears with a bag that holds the lead rope and some brushes and things. She hands the bag to Cid.

I take the bridle from Queenie and place the shiny silver bit gently against Smokey's teeth. He smells wonderful, like newly mown hay and rolled oats. He may be green, but I can tell from his eyes that he's really gentle. He snorts softly, then opens his mouth to take the bit. I pull the bridle up, fumbling with his ears because I'm nervous about spooking him, and then I fasten the chin strap.

Once I have all the straps done up properly, I cluck softly to get him to come along. Smokey hangs back for a bit, then walks on. I cluck again and lead him from the paddock. I don't take the time to admire him or check his feet or anything, because I'm afraid those kids will change their minds and want him back. But they just sit on the fence rail, saying nothing. I can't believe they would let total strangers walk away with their pony. I know that Queenie is thinking the same thing, and secretly, we don't care. If those kids didn't take to Smokey, they *should* give him to some kids who will. And that's us.

"Thank you," I say to the woman.

She smiles and nods. "Take care."

And that's that. I can't believe how easy it was.

the ride home

I take the reins and walk Smokey through the gate and down the lane. Queenie is skipping along next to me. We haven't even hit the road when Cid starts in about how she wants to ride him.

"You have to wait. I don't want them to see us riding him in case Smokey kicks up and one of us falls off."

"You're not the boss of everything," Cid says.

At this point I want to hit her with the reins, because I know it would hurt a lot. "Just *wait* until they can't see us," I hiss at her, my eyes squinting. She can see that I'm serious and backs off.

Queenie is walking with one hand on Smokey's neck. She hasn't said a thing, but her eyes are as wide as saucers. I run my hand along the pony's neck. I can feel his muscles moving in an easy rhythm as he walks. His eyes are dark and kind, and his nostrils are bright pink and dewy on the inside.

When we can't see the farm anymore, I tell Cid she can ride him. "I'll hold the reins while you get on."

She hands me the bag of brushes, then swings her leg up. Smokey quickly steps to one side. Cid hops on one foot like a pogo stick, her other leg still slung halfway over Smokey's back.

"Hold him still!" she says angrily.

"Just hurry up and get on!" I tell her, and then I talk to Smokey the way cowboys do in the movies. "Whoa now, easy, boy." I stroke his muzzle for extra assurance. He snorts and tosses his head. He doesn't know what to think. I rub his forelock and talk softly in his ear until Cid slings herself up. Smokey's back legs buckle slightly as he considers her weight. I hold the reins near the bit and hand the rest over Smokey's head to Cid. When I let go, Smokey lays his ears flat. I can tell he doesn't like the idea. Cid taps his sides with her heels—and the ride is on!

Smokey springs forward, then steps quickly to one

side. His back legs compress, and then he prances like a Lipizzaner. Queenie watches with her big eyes. Cid holds the reins tightly with one hand and clutches a handful of Smokey's mane with the other. She keeps her legs pressed to Smokey's sides. Her teeth are clenched and her face is serious. I have to admit I'm impressed with her guts—really impressed—but I would never tell her that.

"Give him another little kick," I say, when Smokey stops. Cid kicks him, and he lunges forward again.

Despite all the snorting and stamping, Smokey never goes really wild. I can tell by his eyes that he feels obliged to put up a bit of a fuss—for dignity's sake—but that his heart isn't mean at all. He soon settles and gets used to the idea of the weight on his back. He walks quickly, blowing through flared nostrils and swinging his head from side to side. His mane dances up and down and his tail streams out behind him like a comet. Queenie trots beside him, her hand against his neck like she's afraid to let go in case he disappears into the summer air like a mirage.

By the time Cid lets me on him, Smokey is pretty much broke. He doesn't try to step away when I get on, but stands and waits for me to gather the reins. He whinnies loudly while he waits, and I can feel the air pushing through him, his sides quivering against my legs. His coat is soft and warm, and I fit comfortably behind his withers like he was made for me. I give him a nudge with my heels, and he lurches forward, picking along the gravel road with quick, even steps.

The sunlight is fading now. We move in and out of the shadows, the trees casting long dark bands across the road. I am so happy, I feel like I could ride forever. I want to keep following the sun until we reach the ocean. I would ride through the waves that foam and crash against the sand.

Then I remember Queenie. She's been waiting so patiently for her turn, her small hand still resting against the pony's neck as she trots alongside him. "You get on now, Queenie," I say, reining Smokey to a stop. I jump off and hold him by the bridle. I grab Queenie and push her up, then hand her the reins. I give a *cluck, cluck* with my tongue, and Smokey gets up, moving smoothly forward. I stay close, just in case, and I watch Queenie. "How do you like it up there, Queenie?"

Queenie's whole face smiles. Her eyes glow as she watches Smokey. I think she looks like an angel riding that white pony, the sunlight shining behind her, the little tendrils from her wheat-colored braids shimmering around her face.

I'm watching Queenie like this when something awful happens. From out of nowhere, we are attacked by a big, stupid dog. It charges out of the woods and hits us like a freight train. A Bouvier, I think. I don't know what a dog like that is doing out in the middle of the country. It must have broken off its leash or its owners let it out and forgot about it, but at this point it doesn't matter. The dog is snapping and growling like it's rabid or possessed, and suddenly there's a mess of fangs and black fur all over Smokey. I grab the reins as Smokey rears into the air to get away. He spins around squealing, Queenie holding on to his mane with both hands, her face frozen in fear. I can hear my heart pounding in my ears. Cid is yelling and lashing at the dog with the chain on the end of the lead rope. I'm kicking at the dog. Smokey is kicking, too, his back legs thumping on the dog again and again. It's yelping and snarling like crazy. I feel a sharp pain in my left leg but I keep kicking anyway. Before I know it, the reins break free from my hand with a jerk that almost pulls my arm from its socket. Smokey bolts down the road, the reins whipping in front of his legs, the dog tearing after him like the devil.

"Hold on, Queenie!" I shout.

But it's too late. She hits the ground like a rag doll. Smokey and the dog disappear over a hump in the road and are gone.

Cid and I run to where Queenie is lying on the road. Her eyes are closed and she's struggling to breathe. "Queenie, are you hurt?" I ask her. My mind is racing. I can see blood on the side of her face, and I'm scared.

"Do something!" Cid screams at me.

"Queenie, get up," I say, pushing on her shoulder.

Queenie moans and her eyes flutter. "The pony . . ."

"Sit up, Queenie," I tell her, trying to sound strong even though my voice is cracking. "The pony is fine. We'll get him in a bit."

"Ma's gonna kill us," Cid says.

"Shut up!" I snap.

Queenie's eyes flutter some more. I put my arm around her waist and pull her up. Her face twists in pain. Her lip is cut and bleeding. When I finally get her to stand, I see that there is something seriously wrong. There is a lump on her collarbone, and the skin has already turned blue—from the blood underneath, I think. I'm not a doctor, but I can tell this isn't good.

"Oh, God," Cid whispers.

I scowl at her, and she knows enough to be quiet. She hugs the brushes to her chest, tears welling up in her eyes. I give her another look because I don't want her to start crying and make everything worse.

"That was some good riding, Queenie," I say, trying to take her mind off the pain.

"Where's the pony?" Queenie murmurs.

"He's just over the hill," I lie, for the second time in one day. It seems lying gets easier the more you do it. Or maybe there are no half measures when it comes to lies—either you're a liar or you're not.

We weave drunkenly down the road, me supporting Queenie, Cid clutching at her stomach, trying to keep the tears from coming. We're in a real mess now, that's for sure. I try to imagine what Luke Skywalker would do in a situation like this, but I can't think of a single thing. Han Solo was better at tight situations anyway, but that doesn't help matters. For some reason I have KC and the Sunshine Band's "Keep It Comin' Love" playing in a loop through my head.

As we reach the top of the road, I am thankful to

see Smokey standing at the bottom of the hill, just like I promised Queenie. His eyes are wild. The dog is nowhere to be seen, and I'm glad. I hope Smokey managed to kick it senseless.

"Look, Queenie," I say brightly. "Smokey's right there waiting for us, just like I said."

This seems to make her feel better. We shuffle toward the pony, and all I can think is, *Thank you, Smokey, for not trying to run back home.* How would I have explained that to the lady? He doesn't bolt when I walk up to him, but leans his head against my chest as though he's known me since he was a colt. I run my hand along his neck and down his legs, one after the other. There are some scratches and marks, but mostly he's fine.

"Do you think you can get back on him?" I ask Queenie. "I'll lead him this time. It will be fine. You have to get back on a horse if you've been thrown, so he knows you aren't afraid." That's the truth, but it isn't why I said it. I'm really hoping that Queenie isn't as hurt as she seems and that she'll just get on the pony like before. If I can convince her to get back on Smokey, maybe everything will be OK.

But she doesn't need convincing. Like I said, of the

three of us, Queenie wants the pony most of all. Cid holds the reins while I help Queenie up. Queenie cries out because of her collarbone, but she doesn't make a big deal of it, and soon we're moving along the road at a good pace.

ghosts

Despite the trouble we're in, we all start thinking about what we're going to do with Smokey.

"Where are we going to keep him, Nathaniel?" Cid asks.

I don't say a thing. There's a long, loud silence.

"How about the shed out back?" Queenie mumbles.

"We can't keep him in the backyard," Cid says in frustration. "It's not legal. We don't have anywhere to keep him, Nathaniel. We're screwed."

"No, we're not," I finally say. "I was thinking up at Forest Road."

"Clem's barn?" Cid gasps. "Oh, Nathaniel, no! I don't want to see that awful pig man ever again!"

The pig man. He *was* awful. We knew him from when we were little kids living in the big stone house up on Forest Road. When we first moved to East-view, we rented that house. Dad was around then. Clem lived in the barn down the lane. He lived no better than an animal out there with those pigs. He used to chase us with a bullwhip when he caught us playing in the hay. We never told Ma that.

"He's dead and you know it. He fell off a beam and broke his neck."

"What if his ghost is there?" Cid asks. "That's what everybody says. People hear him in there, and someone even said they heard his pigs squealing."

"His ghost is *not* there. If he had a soul at all, it's suffering in hell. Nothing as nice as a horse barn. Besides, we have no choice. It's the cheapest place around. Clem is dead and gone. Ted Henry owns the barn. If we pay board, no one can stop us from being there. Not Clem's ghost or anyone else."

We all think about this for a while, walking for a very long time without saying anything. As we're walking, I look over my shoulder from time to time. Queenie's face is pinched and white as milk, and this reminds me that we're in big trouble. I don't even know if Ted Henry will let us keep Smokey in his barn, but I can't afford to think like that now. I remember the pain in my leg and look down to see that my pants are torn below the knee. My leg looks all scraped and it stings, but that's the least of my worries. It's getting darker and darker, and the trees are starting to blur into big blobs at the side of the road. I can see stars poking through the sky and a sliver of moon pushing up through the branches.

"My feet hurt," Cid groans.

I want to be mad at her for being selfish, but for some reason I can't. I look up at Queenie, who sits hunched over the pony. Smokey is walking with his eyes half closed, his soft breath a warm pulse against my hand. "We're almost there."

Sure enough, the gravel road soon becomes asphalt and we are on the edge of town.

"You'll have to get down now, Queenie," I say. "Ted Henry's house is just up the street, and I have to talk to him about board."

Queenie winces and sucks in her breath as I help her down. I kiss her on the forehead the way Ma always does, then lead Smokey across the road, Queenie and Cid walking beside me. The cars and lights make

Smokey nervous. He tosses his head from side to side. I hold him tighter, just to be sure he doesn't bolt.

On the sidewalk in front of Ted Henry's house I hand the reins to Cid. "You and Queenie stay here while I go talk to him." I try to sound confident when I say this, but I can't help feeling nervous.

I walk up the stairs to the house and bang on the door. I wait for a bit and bang again. No answer. I look around at Cid and Queenie and shrug. Their faces are pale and grim in the light. I'm just about to bang a third time when the door opens with a *whoosh*.

Ted Henry is standing in front of me, sucking his teeth as though I pulled him away from the dinner table. He's wearing a Labatt Blue T-shirt and a worn black baseball cap over his fuzzy brown hair. His fingers are stained brown with nicotine. He sizes me up, then looks at his watch to make me aware of how late it is. I know it's after nine o'clock because the sun is nearly gone, but it can't be helped.

"Whaddya want?" he says.

"I'd like to rent a stall in your barn," I say as bravely as I can, because I don't like Ted Henry and I'm sure he doesn't like me.

"For what?" he asks, like I'm up to no good.

"For our pony." I wave my arm over at Smokey.

He cranes his head for a look, then sucks his teeth some more. "You got money?"

"Yes, sir." I pull the wad of bills from my pocket.

"Ten dollars a month for a standing stall—no hay," Ted Henry says. "Hay is five dollars extra."

"We don't need hay." This isn't entirely true. We do need hay, but I'm sure I can buy it cheaper somewhere else. If I'm not careful, my money will be gone before I know it.

"I need three month's up front. That's thirty dollars. You got that, boy?"

I peel thirty dollars from my ball of money and hand it to him. He counts it twice, then folds it and puts it in his pocket. He seems pleased about the money, and his voice takes on a different tone.

"First stall in the middle aisle. You can set him up in there."

I thump down the stairs excitedly because I can't believe it worked out. I'm so happy, I almost forget the trouble we're in. Until I look at Queenie's face. You can tell she's in pain, and the lump on her collarbone looks bigger and angrier than before.

"Where did you get all that money?" Cid starts in on me like she always does.

Normally I would come back at Cid with something smart when she jumps on me like this, but I'm too tired for a fight. I just tell her the truth. "I saved it from my paper route. Come on. We have to get Smokey settled and get home as fast as we can."

I help Queenie back onto the pony. She moans a bit, but she doesn't cry. It's a good half mile from Ted Henry's house to the barn. We move as quickly as we can without causing Queenie any more discomfort. While we're walking, a couple of cars slow almost to a stop, then drive on. Cid and I exchange glances.

"They must be looking at Smokey," I say.

When we get to the top of the hill, we stop to stare at our old house on Forest Road. Or what's left of it. A tornado tore the roof off a couple of years after we moved out. Then some kids set fire to it and gutted the insides—at least, what the rain and snow hadn't already destroyed.

We loved that old stone house, even though we only lived there for six months and we all agreed it must be haunted. The cellar had a dirt floor and nobody ever wanted to go down there—not even Ma. Sometimes, late at night, we could hear funny noises and whispers in the walls. Even so, we loved it. It was the first place we ever lived in Canada—back in 1972. Dad rented it for us, when things were still good and hopeful. It was a temporary place to live until our big yellow house was ready on the outskirts of town. We moved to Eastview because Dad was supposed to go partners with his brother in the pool-digging business. They were going to make pots of money, he said. So we left our home and all our relatives and friends in Illinois for some southern Ontario pipe dream of Dad's that never panned out.

There was a shed out back where we kept our ponies, and a small fieldstone house behind, where hired help would have lived in better times. There were two bathrooms in the big house: a huge one with a claw-foot tub and a window that stretched from the floor to the ceiling, and a tiny closet with just a toilet inside. The closet toilet was so small you couldn't even shut the door, because your knees got in the way. There was an old cherry banister in the house that corkscrewed from the top of the stairs to the bottom. The rungs were old and loose, and the banister swayed and creaked like it was going to snap off and break our necks when we slid down for dinner.

I got very sick in the stone house once. I was so

sick, Ma let me sleep in her bed to keep an eye on me. I was delirious with fever and I saw things that weren't there. I thought I saw Dad come through the bedroom door, a big smile on his face, though I knew he was back in the States by then. He brought me different kinds of jelly in little round jars and a small glass paperweight with an American flag inside. The flag was made of red, white, and blue rhinestones that glittered like diamonds. Of course it wasn't real, but it seemed that way at the time. I asked Ma about it for days.

We spent our first Canadian Christmas in this house. Dad got us a Christmas tree that reached right to the ceiling—over twelve feet high! It had tiny pine cones on the ends of its branches, and it was the most beautiful tree we'd ever seen. When I think of it now, I think the tree was Dad's way of saying sorry for what he was going to do, because we didn't see much of him after that. Ma told us he had to stay back in Illinois to sell our place there. So we moved into the big yellow house without him. He came once in a while, but he never stayed for long. I can't help thinking about him now, off with some other woman, having fun with his new family. I don't know if any of this is true. But I feel sick just thinking about it—him having more kids with someone else and leaving us behind. Ma tried as hard as she could to make things OK. She even let us live on peanut-butter-and-honey crackers and milk shakes, which Dad never would have allowed. And then we had to sell the yellow house and move into something more "affordable" in town, which is where we live now.

Smokey tugs on the reins and drags me back from remembering. He's sniffing the air excitedly, smelling the other horses in the barn.

"You'd better get off now, Queenie. Smokey might get a bit crazy when he sees the other horses."

I help her down and slip my hand through the bridle. The other horses hear us and start to whinny. Smokey pricks up his ears and whinnies back. I walk quickly beside him, the horses calling back and forth. When we reach the barn, I stop in front of the door.

"Open it," I say to Cid. "See if you can find the light."

"What if Clem's in there?"

"For Pete's sake, just do it!"

"Why don't you do it?"

"Fine, you big chicken. Come here and hold

Smokey." I hand her the reins, but not without giving her the meanest look yet. "Don't let him go." I lean toward her and cluck like an old hen just to bug her.

Cid frowns but doesn't say anything as she takes the reins.

I walk over to the barn. I fumble with the latch, which is kind of rusty, but finally manage to get it open. I have to admit, I'm scared of seeing Clem, too, but no matter what happens, we have to get Smokey set up for the night. The door opens with a creak and I peer inside. I can hear the horses shifting in their stalls. I reach my hand out along the wall and feel for the switch. Something fuzzy brushes against my arm, and my ears are suddenly filled with a high-pitched scream!

a big mess

I pull my arm back like it's been scalded with boiling water. I think Clem's ghost has hold of me, and I stumble and push away from the door.

"What's happening?" Cid shrieks. "Get out of there!"

My hand is bumped again, but this time I realize it's only a piece of old rope and the scream I heard was my own. "It's nothing—I'm fine," I call out. My heart is pounding like a drum in my chest, so hard it feels like it's going to burst right through my shirt. I reach in again, the rope nudging my hand as I fumble with the switch.

The bulb casts an eerie light across the barn. I look around quickly to make sure Clem isn't glaring down at me from some beam up in the ceiling. The horses stare back at me with curiosity. Clem is nowhere to be seen. A radio is playing softly from somewhere in the back of the barn. I breathe a sigh of relief and laugh at my silliness.

"OK, bring Smokey in."

Cid leads Smokey into the barn, Queenie in tow. She has her hand on Smokey's neck again.

"Let Smokey go," I tell her. "I don't want him hurting you if he gets too excited by the other horses."

Queenie moves over to where I'm standing. Smokey greets the other horses with a low, excited nicker. The horses stretch their necks over their stalls, sniffing the air. We move along the far aisle to reach the stalls in the middle of the barn. A big chestnut gelding with the name Flag tacked over its stall pins back his ears when Smokey walks by. Smokey pays no attention.

I open the stall door, and Cid walks Smokey inside. She lets him sniff around a bit before removing his bridle and halter. The pony is curious and calm, not at all wild like you would expect a stallion to be. He nuzzles the water bowl. It's empty and dry. I push on the mechanism with my hand, but no water comes out.

"What do you expect for ten dollars a month?" I grumble.

Queenie perches like a bird on the edge of a concrete trough while Cid looks for a bucket.

"I'm going to get some hay," I tell them.

"From where?" Cid asks.

"From the loft, where do you think?"

"Did you pay for it?"

I ignore her and climb the rickety ladder to the loft. I have no idea how much hay there will be. There used to be lots of it here when we were kids. When I reach the loft, I let my eyes adjust to the light. I can see the stars through the slats in the barn walls. To my relief, there is a big pyramid of hay stacked almost to the ceiling and lots of loose hay all over the floor—just like I remember. In fact, it's probably the same hay. It's obviously old and smells a bit moldy. I can't believe Ted Henry wanted to charge us for it. I gather a big handful of the loose hay, inspect it for mold, then toss it down the hole to the floor. I find some straw and throw it down, too. By the time I climb down the ladder, Cid has filled Smokey's feed bin with hay and spread the straw on the floor of his stall with her feet. Smokey is drinking out of a red plastic bucket that Cid found and filled with water.

"There's tons of hay up there," I tell her. "No one will even miss it. Besides, half of it is moldy. We'll have to be careful not to feed Smokey any of the rotten stuff."

"You're just going to take it?"

"There's tons of it!"

Cid stares at me reproachfully, then holds up a small wooden box.

"I found this, too," she says.

The brushes and hoof-picks that the daffodil lady gave us are arranged neatly inside. Queenie watches from her perch on the trough, her face pale and serious.

I nod with approval, then sprinkle water on Smokey's hay.

"Can we get him a plaque with his name on it?" Queenie asks. This is the first thing she's said in hours. "There's a lady at the fair who makes them."

"You don't know that she'll be there this year," Cid says.

"We'll get him one," I say. "But we'd better get home now. Smokey is all settled in. He'll be fine until we can come back tomorrow."

I'd like to stay to make sure Smokey is OK, or to look at the other horses, but I know Queenie's collarbone must be sore and we have to get home. Besides, Ma's used to us going off on our own, but we've never been out this late without telling her where we were going.

I secure the latch on the stall. Smokey watches us as we move along the aisle. I stop to admire him one more time. He looks serene and almost unreal standing there. I feel my heart swell up in my chest. I watch him for a little while longer before I click off the light and close the barn door.

We make our way down the lane in silence. I don't think any of us can believe the pony is ours. The whole day seems like a crazy dream. I look over at Queenie. Her lips are pursed, and she's got one hand on her sore shoulder. I put my arm around her waist. "We'll be home soon."

When we reach the road, a passing car slows down, then drives on. Right after that, another car slows down and the driver looks at us, too. Maybe they're wondering why Queenie looks so bad, I think. Or maybe they're just wondering what three kids are doing this far outside of town this late at night. I wave to let them know that we're fine. The second car stops. The driver rolls down her window and sticks her head out.

"You those Estabrooks kids?"

I nod because I know not to talk to strangers.

"You kids are in a heap of trouble. It's all over the radio. The whole town is looking for you. Your mother is worried sick."

The radio? That's why those cars were slowing down to look at us. Now I know we're done. Ma's been worried before, but she's never called the radio station. Usually she just puts on her house robe and starts walking up the street to find us.

"What's wrong with that girl?" the woman demands, pointing at Queenie.

"Nothing. She's fine. We're just on our way home now."

"You'd better get in the car. I don't want your mother worrying anymore."

I hesitate because I'm thinking it might not be safe. Cid looks at me, and we both look at Queenie. "Come on," I say. "It can't get much worse than this."

We shuffle over to the car, and I help Queenie in and snap her seat belt on.

"We live at 251 Light Stree—" I start to say, but the woman cuts me off.

"I know full well where you live. Everyone knows

where you live now. You kids must be out of your minds tearing around till all hours. If you were my kids, I'd teach you a thing or two."

I'm tempted to mouth off, but think better of it. "Yes, ma'am," I say, hoping this will appease her. But it doesn't. She just keeps at us, and I suppose we deserve it.

"It's hard enough trying to keep a house going under the best circumstances, let alone when a woman is fending for herself. You kids must sit around thinking of ways to drive your mother crazy."

She natters on and on like this the whole way home. I nod once in a while to let her know I'm minding, but Cid and Queenie just stare at the floor of the car. I'd like to stare at the floor of the car, too, but somebody has to take responsibility.

To my horror, Ma's waiting on the porch smoking a cigarette. I haven't seen her smoke since we lived in Illinois. She throws the cigarette to the ground and rushes over to the car, pulling the tie of her robe tight around her. I don't have to look at her to tell she's hysterical. I'm not even out of the car before she starts boxing and slapping me on the head.

"What are you trying to do to me? What's the matter with you? I was worried sick. The whole town is out looking for you. I had to call the radio just to find you. Do you know how embarrassed I am? You're just like your father. You're going to kill me!"

I put my hands up to cover my face. I try to explain, but I can't get a word in edgewise with Ma cuffing me like that. She hits me so hard, my ears start to ring and I feel like I'm going to be sick. The woman in the car just sits there watching, and I hate her for being so nosy. I wish she would drive away and leave us alone.

When Ma finally stops hitting me, she bursts into tears. It may sound funny, but this hurts me more than all the slapping and yelling ever could.

"I'm sorry, Ma. We didn't mean to scare you."

Ma's sobbing into her hands like she'll never stop. I've only heard her cry like this once before, and that's when Dad left us. I feel so ashamed, I can't even look at her. Ma keeps sobbing until she sees Queenie.

"Good God, what happened to you, child?" She rushes over to Queenie.

Queenie finally breaks down, because she is tired and scared and she can't be strong anymore, not with Ma crying and all.

"What have you done to her?" Ma screams at me.

"It was an accident. . . . She fell."

Ma runs her hands over Queenie. "My baby, my poor baby . . ."

Cid is crying now, too, but softly, sniffling into her shirt, her face crumpled like an old tin can. She moves over to where I am, and we stand mutely watching.

The woman in the car offers to drive Queenie and Ma to the hospital. They get in the car and drive off, leaving Cid and me standing in front of the house.

i run away

"They've been gone for an awfully long time," Cid says, looking out the living room window. "I hope Queenie is OK. I've never seen Ma so mad before. I thought she was going to kill you."

They *have* been gone a long time. I'm concerned about Queenie, but I have to admit, I'm not in any hurry to face Ma. I don't mind so much that she hit me. I was more embarrassed than anything else. But I'm sorry that I made Ma worry so much. I never want to be like my dad.

While we are waiting for Ma and Queenie to return, I wash my knee in the sink. After the blood is cleaned up, I can see that the dog only grazed the skin. It isn't nearly as bad as it could have been. "We'll have to tell Ma about Smokey when they get back," I say, trying to thread a needle to fix the tear in my pants. My fingers feel like a tangle of thumbs, and the thread goes everywhere except through the needle. Cid grabs it from me and threads it as easily as if the needle were the size of a wooden spoon, then hands it back to me.

"She'll never let us keep him. What are we going to do? We can't take him back. That would be just awful."

"We're not going to take him back. I don't care what Ma says. I know she's mad now, but I'll convince her once she cools down. I have my paper route. She won't have to have any part in it. She doesn't have to pay for a thing." I don't know who I'm trying to convince with this delivery, me or Cid, but it makes me feel better to say it and it seems to make Cid feel better to hear it.

Cid's just about to turn on the TV when we hear the sound of the car crunching the gravel in the driveway. We can hear Ma thanking the woman, then the doors slamming and the car driving off. I take a deep breath, because I'm afraid of what will happen next.

I tie a finishing knot in the thread, then break it with my teeth. My sewing is terrible compared to Ma's. But I sure wasn't going to ask her to mend my pants.

Ma walks in, helping Queenie through the door. Queenie looks tired, but she's smiling. Her eyes are kind of glazed over—probably from the painkillers they gave her at the hospital. She has a small stuffed bear in her hands and a plaster cast that runs thick and white over one shoulder, across her chest, and under her arm. There's a Scooby-Doo sticker on the front of it. Her shirt had been cut to make room for the cast, and she looks like a little football player just coming in from a hard game.

Ma kisses Queenie on the forehead, then walks right past me without saying a word. This is not good. I'm more afraid of her silence than her yelling. Ma can freeze you out forever. Once, she didn't talk to Dad for three months, she was so mad at him for something. I can hear her clattering pots in the kitchen. Cid and I rush over to where Queenie is standing.

"What was wrong with you?" Cid asks. "You're so lucky to have a cast."

"The doctor said I broke my collarbone," Queenie

says, touching the cast reverently. "Feel it. It's hard as anything."

Cid taps lightly on the cast.

"The hospital people were really nice. They gave me this bear and this sticker, too."

"Did it hurt?" Cid asks. "Can I sign your cast?"

"I'm sorry, Queenie," I finally say. "It's my fault. I should have known better."

I don't know what I could have done differently, but it makes me feel better to apologize. I'm proud of Queenie for being so strong. The whole way home with that broken collarbone, she didn't cry once. I feel ashamed all of a sudden and, honestly, just a little bit jealous. If I had broken my collarbone, Ma would be fussing over me instead of hating my guts.

"Ma knows about Smokey," Queenie says softly. "I had to tell her. She didn't say much, but I think she's really mad. She's gonna make us take him back, isn't she, Nat?"

"I won't let her," I say, trying to sound confident, the way I did before with Cid. But somehow, it doesn't come across that way. I know I have to go into the kitchen and talk to Ma. I'd rather have a million needles jabbed in my eyes, but I know I have to do it or the whole thing with Smokey will fall apart. And after all we've been through, I can't let that happen.

I stand in the doorway to the kitchen. Queenie and Cid hover behind me. Ma is mixing something up on the stove. It smells like hot chocolate. Probably for Queenie, since she broke her collarbone and all. Ma has her back to me, and although she's not a big woman, she seems gigantic right now.

"Ma . . ."

She doesn't answer me but just keeps mixing the hot chocolate.

"Ma . . . I want to explain to you—"

"You're taking that horse back tomorrow, Nathaniel."

"It's a pony, Ma, not a horse."

"Pony, horse, I don't care. You're taking it back tomorrow all the same."

"Just let me explain, Ma. The pony didn't cost us a thing—"

"It cost Queenie a collarbone already!"

She's got me there. I stare at the floor. I know I'm going to have to be fast on my feet if I'm going to win her over. "Ma, if you could just see him, you would want us to keep him—I know you would. He's beautiful and white and gentle as a puppy. He's just like a picture, Ma. Queenie loves that pony to death. You know how long she's been waiting to get one. It wasn't Smokey's fault she broke her collarbone."

"It's a God-damned stallion, Nathaniel!"

Ma blindsides me with this one. How did she know Smokey is a stallion? I should have told Queenie not to mention that little detail.

"But he's really gentle, Ma. We were chased by a dog, and Smokey was just trying to get away. It wasn't anybody's fault. It won't cost you anything for us to keep him. I have my paper route to cover the expenses. And with Cid, Queenie, and me taking care of him, he won't be any trouble. You won't have to worry about it at all. I promise."

Ma keeps her back to me. I can see she isn't going to budge, which might explain what I say next.

"You have to let us keep him. That pony is the best thing to happen to us in years. If Dad were here, he'd let us keep him."

This makes Ma turn around, all right, and she looks at me like she's staring at the devil himself. She doesn't yell these next words. She spits them through her teeth.

"I don't want to hear another word. You take that pony back tomorrow."

"Please, Ma—"

"Get out and leave me alone!"

Ma's words hit me like broken glass. I feel the anger rise up inside me, and before I know what's happening, I'm screaming. "I hate you! I won't take the pony back! Not tomorrow or ever! Dad left because of you, and I don't blame him, you old witch!"

Ma stares at me, her jaw dropped, the wooden spoon she was using to stir the cocoa still held in the air. Queenie and Cid just stand there, their faces all shocked and disbelieving. I slam out the mudroom door and stumble down the stairs in my bare feet. I feel like a big fist is hitting me in the stomach. I think I'm going to throw up. I start to run and I keep running, past the corner store and through the park. I run past rows and rows of houses that all look the same, past the church and the jailhouse. I run until I'm far away from everything and my lungs feel like they're going to burst.

I keep running, but no matter how fast I go, I can't outrun the image of Ma's face. The terrible words stab at my brain over and over. I collapse on the lawn of a house where the windows are dark, and then I start to cry like I have never cried before. I can't stop my body from shaking. "I'm not like my f-father. I'm not like my father."

A light snaps on at the side of the house. I pick myself up and walk out into the street. I follow the road to the edge of town, walking up the big hill until I am standing at the end of the lane that leads to the barn. It's dark, and I have to be careful. The gravel in the lane is sharp, and I have to stop several times to brush the stones from the soles of my feet.

When I reach the barn, I feel for the latch. It opens with a *click,* and I close the door behind me. I don't even care if Clem's ghost is in here. It's better than being at home, I think. I can hear the horses stirring in their stalls. They must wonder what I'm doing here so late. I can see Smokey's white shape. He nickers softly.

"It's OK, Smokey."

I don't bother opening the door to his stall, but climb over the side instead, using the edge of the old concrete feed trough as a boost up. Smokey is soft and warm. He rubs his head on my sleeve and gently nibbles my finger. For some reason this makes me feel like crying all over again. Smokey nudges my hand as though he understands. I just stand there enjoying his warmth for a long time before I curl up in the straw in one corner of the stall. My feet are burning from the walk. Smokey looks at me with curiosity and chews his hay. Then he walks over and sniffs me, placing a hoof lightly on my leg.

"You're a good boy, Smokey. I won't take you back, no matter what Ma says."

I feel a shiver run up my spine. I think it must be Clem, trying to haunt me out of his barn. For a moment I'm afraid and I wish I was in my own bed, staring up at the ceiling and watching the spider mend her web in the corner of my room. I feel smaller than I ever have in my life. I imagine myself dead and think about how sorry Ma will be when she sees me laid out in a coffin. I imagine everyone walking past me, my skin all blue and my hands neatly folded across my chest. Then I start to wonder if anybody came to Clem's funeral, or if he even had a funeral. I think about what he must have looked like, lying on the barn floor, his neck broken, his stained teeth biting into his swollen tongue. I spook myself again thinking about his ghost whirling around in the rafters of the barn. I can feel my heart start to beat faster, but then I open my eyes and look at Smokey. His quiet dignity comforts me as he calmly chews his hay, and somehow I manage to fall asleep—sore feet, ghosts, and all.

I don't know how long I've been sleeping when I hear someone calling my name. At first I think I'm dreaming, but then Cid's voice startles me.

"Nathaniel!"

"Cid! What are you doing here?"

"I knew you'd be here. I came to tell you to come home. Ma sent me. She says we can keep Smokey."

"What?"

"Queenie and I talked to her. She was really upset when you left, but we talked to her and now everything's OK. We explained about the money and how you paid for the stall. You know Ma can't deny Queenie anything."

I'm so happy to hear Cid's words that I spring up over the stall and throw my arms around her. I know it doesn't seem right for a brother to hug his sister, especially a boss like Cid, but I'm so glad to hear the news, I'm really not thinking straight.

"Where are your shoes?" she asks.

I look down at my feet. My dirty toes wiggle back at me. "I didn't wear any."

Cid looks at me funny and then laughs. I'm embarrassed, but I laugh a bit, too.

We tend to Smokey for a while, and Cid tells me the whole story about what happened after I ran out of the house. Ma must have been pretty worried to allow Cid to walk here this late at night by herself, and this makes me feel terrible again. I take my time in the barn, because I'm loath to leave Smokey behind, and, to be honest, I'm not looking forward to seeing Ma. I know everything is fine now, but there's an awful thing that comes with feeling sorry and that's the fear of facing the one you've wronged. I'm sure the words I said to Ma are still echoing in the air back home.

Before we go, we walk through the barn, looking at all the horses. There is a big quarter horse mare named Silver, a Morgan colt named Rush, a couple of skinny palominos with no names, an old rodeo buckskin named Pip, and the big chestnut named Flag. At the very back of the barn in a room off by itself is a huge black gelding named Jed. He has a Roman nose and wild eyes. He snorts through the rungs of his stall, pacing restlessly back and forth.

"He doesn't have any hay," Cid says.

I look at the tack box by the stall. It has Ted Henry's name roughly gouged into the wood. "Figures," I mumble. I get a few flakes of hay from the loft and push them into Jed's bin. I get some water and pour it into his bucket, then sprinkle a bit on the hay. When Cid is satisfied that Jed is comfortable, we're ready to leave.

As we walk home, I play out the impending scene with Ma over and over in my head. But no matter how many times I run it through my mind, I still feel bad. Cid walks along like everything's fine, because for her, it is. She didn't say those terrible words. She talks about *Star Wars* and how she'd like to see it again and how there's this kid in town who's seen the movie over a hundred times and the people at the movie theater don't even charge him to see it anymore. She goes on and on like this until we reach the house. I hesitate before opening the door.

"Wait a minute, Nat," Cid says. Then she does the nicest thing she's ever done. She reaches over and gently brushes some straw from my hair and smoothes it on both sides with her hands. "OK."

Ma is waiting in the kitchen when I come in. She's sitting at the table, her face sober, her eyes swollen and red.

"Ma . . ." I start to say, but she waves me quiet.

She speaks like she's been rehearsing the words all night. "I don't blame you for the way you feel, Nathaniel. I've tried really hard to make a life for you kids. I've tried hard to make up for Dad leaving. I guess I fooled myself into thinking that things with you kids were all right, that I'd managed to—"

"Ma, it's not your fault—" I say, but she quiets me again. She adjusts the tie on her house robe, and I'm afraid she's going to start to cry, but she doesn't.

"I've been thinking long and hard about that pony. I was so upset with you kids being lost, I wasn't thinking straight. And when I saw Queenie, I almost died. You're a young man, Nathaniel, and I trust that you will be responsible."

"I will, Ma. I've got it all figured out. . . ."

"If you feel you can be responsible, then you can keep the pony. I've really tried to make things OK for you kids—"

Her voice cracks and I can't take any more. I rush over to where she's sitting and throw myself at her feet. And even though I'm twelve, I bury my head in her lap the way I used to when I was a little kid, and it's me who starts to cry. "Oh, Ma, I'm sorry. I'm so sorry."

a violent battle

Queenie isn't allowed to go to the barn until her collar-bone is mended. That'll be a good month or so. She's sore as anything about this fact but knows better than to fight with Ma after all we've been through. The crazy thing is, in the days Cid and I have been riding our skateboards to the stable together, we haven't fought once. She's even stopped bugging me about taking hay all the time to feed Smokey. I know she hates that I take it without paying, but she understands now that we have to do it to save money. Anyway, I never thought I'd say this, but Cid and I are actually getting along.

"What do you think his show name should be?" she asks.

"How about Smoker's Cough?" I say, just kidding around. We laugh hard about this, our skateboards grinding loudly over the pavement.

While we're riding and laughing and generally enjoying each other's company, Cid tells me a funny story that she never told anyone before. She tells me how she got her skateboard. I bought mine with my paper-route money. It's all purple with swirls of different colors. Cid saw it and wanted one, too, but had to save and save for ages—birthday money and such. When she finally had enough money, she took the bus to the mall. She bought an orange skateboard, just like mine. She had just enough for the skateboard and her bus fare home. But Cid had a taste for candy that day and spent half her fare on some licorice and red hots. When the bus pulled up, she got on with her new skateboard under her arm, threw the loose change in the slot, and started to walk to the back of the bus. The bus driver stopped her with a shout and told her to ante up. Cid ends up giving him some sob story about being left at the mall by her parents and how she didn't have enough money to get home and wouldn't he please just take her as far as

67

town—all of this with a mouth full of candy! And he did! I didn't know Cid had it in her!

When we get to the top of the hill, we kick our skateboards and carry them down the lane to the barn. The door is open.

"Must be somebody here," I say.

"Who do you think it is?"

"I don't know. But we'll find out."

No sooner do we step into the barn than we're assaulted by a loud voice.

"You kids own this stallion?"

I let my eyes adjust for a second, and a big, red-faced man with a baseball cap comes into view. It's not Ted Henry. Except for the cap, he looks and sounds like a hairy gorilla. "Yes, sir, we do."

"You've got some nerve bringing a stallion into this barn. We've got mares in heat in here and he's going to go crazy!"

Cid and I look over at Smokey calmly chewing his hay.

"Mister, he wouldn't hurt a flea."

"Son, I won't tell you again. You'd better get that stallion gelded or there'll be hell to pay. I don't want some balls-crazy pony spooking the other horses!"

I stifle a snicker at his use of "balls-crazy." I've never heard an adult talk like this before. This doesn't help the matter at all.

"You think this is funny, son? I have a mind to throw you and your pony out into the street. You'd better take care of this situation, pronto!"

"Yes, sir," I say, just to get the Gorilla off my back. "It's already been arranged."

This seems to satisfy him, and he stomps out of the barn without another word. I follow him to the door and close it after him.

"Who the heck was that?" Cid asks.

"Some big jerk who thinks he knows everything."

"What are we going to do? What if he does throw Smokey out into the street?"

"He won't do anything of the kind," I say, but secretly I'm worried he's already gone ratting us out to Ted Henry.

"What are we going to do, Nat?"

"I don't know. That gorilla can't make us do anything." I have to admit, I don't like the idea of getting Smokey gelded. I don't think any boy likes the idea of anything being treated that way—for obvious reasons. The Gorilla doesn't know Smokey. He doesn't know that Smokey wouldn't cause any trouble. I don't think Smokey even knows he's a stallion.

I'm thinking like this as I lead Smokey out of the barn to the small field where the horses are allowed to graze. The Morgan colt named Rush presses his face against the bars of his stall. He's the only horse other than Jed who's left in the barn on this beautiful day. I realize then that the Gorilla owns the colt. I consider letting him out, then think better of it. We don't need any more trouble. I rub the colt's nose as Smokey and I walk past.

The other horses are grazing happily in the field. Smokey whinnies excitedly when he sees them. He isn't off the lead for more than two seconds when the big chestnut named Flag comes charging over, his mane and tail flying, his big yellow teeth bared.

"Oh, no! Smokey, look out!" Cid yells.

But it's too late. Flag grabs Smokey by the withers and practically lifts him off the ground. Smokey squeals and rears up. And then he does something that neither Cid nor I can believe. He grabs the horse by the front leg with his teeth and pulls him down to the ground. Flag topples like an old building. He flounders helplessly in the dirt while Smokey trots away victoriously, his mane and tail streaming behind him.

"I can't believe it!" I yell. "He took that horse out without even trying!" I'm so proud I'm busting my shirt buttons, as Dad used to say.

"I guess we don't have to worry about him," Cid says incredulously.

By the time Flag scrambles to his feet, Smokey is already grazing comfortably halfway down the field. The other horses eye him curiously, then continue to graze. Flag walks to the far end of the field, his head hung in defeat. He doesn't even look at Smokey again. We decide that Smokey can hold his own, so we leave him to fend for himself.

Before we go, we check on Jed. I tell Cid to fill up his water bucket and to be careful not to get too close. The horse looks so neglected and wild, he just might bite out of fear. I toss some hay into his feed bin, and we watch him eat for a while in silence.

On the way home, Cid and I can't stop talking about how Smokey took Flag down. We can't believe he had it in him, him being so gentle, and decide it might be a good idea to find a vet and ask about getting him gelded, after all.

When we get to town, we stop in front of a small hand-painted sign that says SMYTH VETERINARY: LARGE ANIMAL PRACTICE. The sign hangs over a set of stairs that leads down to an office below another shop.

"Looks as good as any," I say.

We carry our skateboards down the stairs and into the office. A friendly young man with a smiling, round face and what looks like Fisher-Price snap-on hair is sitting behind the counter. He wears a pair of dirty blue coveralls with some syringes sticking out of the pockets. The room smells like medicine and antiseptic. There are papers and things all over the desk, and the office is generally untidy.

"Can I help you?" the friendly man asks.

"We want to see about getting our pony gelded," I say.

"Who needs a pony gelded?" another man asks, appearing through a doorway.

He's the spitting image of the first man and I think I'm seeing double. I look back and forth at the two men, then turn to look at Cid, who's doing the exact same thing. The men burst out laughing.

"We're twins," the one behind the counter says.

"You both vets?" I ask.

The men nod, smiling.

"Where's your pony at?" the second one asks.

"Up on Forest Road. How much does it cost to have a pony gelded?"

"Well . . . it's a pretty straightforward procedure," the first one says. "For a pony, it's a hundred dollars even."

Cid shoots me a look that says, *Where are we going to get a hundred dollars?* but I don't miss a beat. "When can you do it?"

The first vet flips through his schedule book. "How about this Saturday?"

I tell him sure, and we agree on a time. "You both going to do it?"

"We always work together," the first vet says.

"OK. Well, I guess we'll see you Saturday, then."

"See you Saturday."

As we're walking up the stairs, I can't help thinking that those vet brothers seemed amused by us. I guess there aren't many kids who come in looking to have their pony gelded. Parents usually arrange that sort of thing. But then, there aren't too many vets that have a twin to work with side by side. So I guess we amused each other.

"Where are we gonna get a hundred dollars?" Cid asks as soon as we hit street level.

"I already thought about that," I say in a confident voice, so Cid won't ask me a thousand questions. "I can collect for two weeks instead of one. I'll tell people I'm going on vacation or something and have to collect for two so I can keep the books straight until I get back. You do that sometimes if you have to get another kid to deliver for you and you don't want to trust them with collecting. I'll add that to the money I have saved and that should be enough."

"But what happens when they see you delivering the paper anyway?"

"I'll just tell them that we couldn't go on vacation, after all. Something came up and we couldn't get away."

Cid looks at me like she isn't sure how good an idea this is, but I start to whistle and jump on my skateboard, so she doesn't have a chance to shoot down my plan. To be honest, I'm not sure the plan will work either, but I have to get the money from somewhere, and that's the only idea I can come up with.

When we get home, Queenie is sitting on the couch watching *Charlie's Angels*. It's a rerun. I let Cid tell about Smokey and Flag. Queenie asks all kinds of questions, and Cid does a pretty good job

74

answering them. When she's through, I tell Queenie about getting Smokey gelded.

"Why, Nat? Smokey is as gentle as anything. He doesn't need to be gelded."

"We have to. We won't be allowed to stay in the barn if we don't. And besides, after seeing how he handled himself today, he may have more stallion in him than we think."

Queenie considers this for a minute and then insists on coming.

"Don't talk to me," I tell her. "Talk to Ma. She's the one who doesn't want you hanging around the barn with your cast and all."

"It doesn't even hurt anymore," Queenie protests. She knocks hard on the cast. "See? It's so unfair that I have to stay home while you and Cid have all the fun. I hate this stupid cast!"

"Tell it to Ma. Not me."

By the time Saturday rolls around I can hardly keep myself together. I count my money three times over. I only have eighty-two dollars. I had trouble convincing some of the people to pay me for two weeks in advance, but mostly they were pretty good about it. One woman even offered to pay me for three weeks. I think she was upset on account of

Elvis Presley up and dying like that. One minute he was on tour and the next he was in the hospital and then he was dead. Heart failure, the papers said. I'm not a fan of his music, but Dad used to like him. Anyway, I told the woman three weeks wasn't necessary, even though I could have used the money. I felt too guilty to take it. Another woman, Mrs. Geeter, flat-out refused to pay me for papers she hadn't gotten yet. But she's an old biddy anyway. Always fussing about how I fold the papers and how I put them in her mailbox. She even complains to me about the price, which I have nothing to do with. I just hope the vets don't mind me paying them the rest later. I don't tell Queenie and Cid I haven't got all the money. It would just worry them.

Cid, Queenie, and I get going early so we can be ready when the twins arrive at the barn. Ma fusses a bit and doesn't want to let Queenie go, but Queenie is so determined that Ma caves in and says OK. Ma makes us swear we'll be careful. I promise her everything will be fine. Queenie wears one of my old sweatshirts to cover her cast. The sleeves hang way past her hands.

"Roll those sleeves up so you don't look funny," I tell her.

We can't skateboard to the barn because of Queenie and her cast, but I don't mind. I feel sorry for her missing out on all the excitement so far. It takes us over an hour to walk there. Smokey is waiting for us in his stall when we arrive. Cid and I brought him in from the field the night before and took away his hay and water so he would be ready for the twins this morning.

Queenie sits on the edge of the old feed trough while Cid and I groom Smokey. "Hotel California" drifts over the radio.

"I hate this song," Cid says.

"Yeah. Me, too."

We work away for a while, until we hear a truck pull up next to the barn.

"Hall-o!" a man's voice calls in through the door.

"I'll be right out," I call back.

Cid grabs Smokey's halter and snaps it on. I let her lead him out of the stall. One of the twins sticks his head through the door. "Is that the pony? You can bring him out front here."

Cid leads Smokey out of the barn, and one of the twins takes him by the halter and leads him over to where the equipment is laid out on a blue paper sheet on the ground. There is a big syringe full of something, a stack of gauze pads, several pairs of latex gloves, a bottle of iodine, some alcohol, and a scalpel. Queenie sees the scalpel and gives me a scared look. I wink at her, even though I don't feel so sure myself. I shake the twins' hands the way Dad would have done, and thank them for coming out this far.

"He's a really nice pony," one says.

"What's that for?" Queenie asks, pointing to the big syringe.

"Anesthetic. It'll keep him calm during the proce-dure."

"Will it hurt?"

"No. It won't hurt him a bit. It's very quick."

One of the twins injects Smokey, and I know there's no turning back now. He pets Smokey until the pony's eyes go droopy and his head starts to hang. Smokey looks like a big puppy dog with his head leaning against the vet's thigh.

The other twin puts on a pair of gloves. He wipes Smokey with a gauze pad soaked in alcohol, then douses him with iodine. He picks up the scalpel and starts to cut. Smokey stands patiently. He doesn't even shift his weight. The vet works away for a while, and I'm starting to get nervous. It seems to be taking a long time. He leans one hand on Smokey's flank and leaves a bloody handprint on his hindquarters. I'm thinking Smokey looks like an Indian pony with that red handprint, when I suddenly notice that Cid's face is white and Queenie has tears streaming silently down her cheeks. I put my arm around Queenie to make her feel better.

"It's OK. Smokey can't feel a thing."

Queenie stands there for a bit, then disappears into the barn. The twins look at me to see if everything is OK. I nod back but my somber face gives me away.

"It's done," the vet says, pulling off his gloves and rolling the instruments up in the blue paper sheet. "He's going to be drowsy for a while, but that will wear off soon enough. Keep an eye on him for a day or two and call us if you have any questions."

I pull the wad of money from my jeans and hand it to one of the twins. "It's only eighty-two dollars," I say in a low voice so Cid won't hear. "I can pay the rest as soon as I get paid again—if that's all right with you."

The vet stuffs the wad in his coveralls without even counting it. "Pay the rest when you can," he says. The twins pack up their things in their

79

truck and wave as they drive down the lane. They didn't write me a bill or anything, so I figure they must trust me.

I get Cid to hold Smokey, and I go into the barn. I grab a little bottle of bleach that I saw in the Gorilla's tack box. Queenie is sitting on the old trough, her face stained with tears.

"Is it over?"

"It's over and he's fine. I'm just going to clean him up."

Queenie follows me outside. I take the bleach and an old rag I found in the barn and scrub at the bloody handprint on Smokey's flank. I get most of it off but there's still a thin red shadow of a hand that won't go away. I give up after a while because I'm afraid I'll irritate his skin with the bleach. He's still really drowsy when I lead him back into his stall. I tie him to his feed bin because I'm afraid he'll try to lie down and get straw and dust in his incision.

"Do you think he knows what we did to him?" Queenie asks.

"No. He won't even know the difference," I say, but my words sound hollow. Deep inside I think we've taken something away from him, something essential and necessary. I'm worried that he'll never be the same and that the light will never shine in his dark eyes again.

We wait with Smokey for hours until he seems a little livelier. While we're waiting, Cid feeds and waters Jed. We do this every day now, because as far as we can see, no one ever comes in to take care of him. I guess Ted Henry must come in from time to time, but we've never seen him.

We sit and watch Smokey for a while. Then Cid says we'd better get home before Ma starts to worry about what has happened. Queenie doesn't want to go and neither do I, but we know Cid is right.

I untie Smokey from the rail and remove his halter. He rubs his head against my stomach. I pet him for a bit, then secure the latch to his stall. I give him a long look before closing the barn door.

Smokey recovers fine from his operation, although I can't seem to get over my guilt. I tell myself that it was necessary, that we would have been thrown out of the barn if we didn't do it, or that the stallion's true nature would have caused us trouble in the end, but none of this makes me feel any better. I should have stood up to the Gorilla. I hate myself for letting him force us into doing something we didn't want to do.

To make matters worse, that old biddy Mrs. Geeter eventually catches up with me when she realizes that I didn't go on vacation. She appears at her door like a woodchuck from its hole, just as I'm getting ready to toss her paper.

"Don't you dare throw that paper, you infernal liar!" she yells, for the whole neighborhood to hear.

Her wrinkled lips keep flapping even after she's done yelling, and I can't help thinking that she's got a really loud voice for someone so small and old. I go warily up the walk to hand her the paper, but before I can do this, she snatches it from me and wallops me over the head with it.

"Try to cheat me! I have a mind to call the authorities!"

Of course, that's the last thing I want her to do, so I apologize profusely and promise never to throw her paper again. My apology doesn't seem to make a difference, because she seems to be getting madder by the minute. But just when I think she's going to chase me down the walk, she pops back through her door and is gone.

Despite Mrs. Geeter, I finally manage to collect the money I owe the twins and take it to their office one day on my way to the barn. The brothers look at me again with great amusement.

"How's the pony doing?" one of them asks me.

I tell him that Smokey is fine. I thank him for being patient and giving me time to pay.

"Were you the one who was crying?"

I look at him in surprise. "That was my sister Queenie. She's a girl."

The vet just chuckles and for some reason this irritates me, so I thank the brothers and leave before I'm tempted to say something I will regret.

a different kind of trouble

Before we know it, it's the end of August and time
for the Eastview Fair. This means summer is almost
over and the evil known as school will soon begin.
Queenie's cast is ready to come off now, too, which is
a good thing because she'll be able to come with Cid
and me to take care of Smokey. We've been taking
turns riding Smokey in the field on sunny days, and
when it rains we ride him up and down the aisles in
the barn. The other horses found this interesting at
first, but now they don't even look up when we do
it. No one ever seems to come to the barn—at least,
not while we're there—so we pretty much have
the run of the place. Occasionally the Gorilla shows

up, or one of the women who own the palominos, but we just mind our own business and stay out of their way.

Queenie begs Ma to take her to the doctor to remove her cast before we go to the fair. She says she doesn't want to be "encumbered" while strolling through the fairgrounds. Ma agrees and we take a taxi to the hospital. Cid and I read magazines in the waiting room while Queenie and Ma go in to see the doctor. It isn't long before Queenie reappears holding the pieces of her cast. Her shoulder looks skinny and sallow.

"Look," she says, holding up the cast. "He cut it off with a giant pair of snips."

We admire the cast and inspect her shoulder.

"Looks as good as ever," I say.

After the hospital, Ma walks us over to the fairgrounds. She gives us two dollars each for rides and ice cream. I don't have the heart to tell her it's three dollars just to get through the gate. I tell her not to worry about us if we're late, because we'll probably go to the barn after the fair. Ma just nods. Like I said, she doesn't really mind what we do. It's not that she doesn't care. She's just busy and would rather leave us to our own devices, which is fine by me.

We wait until Ma is out of sight before running along the length of the fence and hopping over behind the horse barns. I help Queenie over the fence, just in case. I don't want her hurting her shoulder so soon after getting her cast removed. We brush ourselves off, then stroll through one of the barns, admiring the horses. There are giant Percherons and Clydesdales calmly eating hay while their owners brush them. There are tiny miniature horses decorated with ribbons and braid. There are quarter horses and pintos and paints, perfectly groomed and waiting to compete in the games.

"Let's go see the lady who makes the plaques," I say.

We weave through the fair, the whirling rides and the loud barkers calling out to us. There are kids running all over, carrying big stuffed toys their fathers won for them. Disco blasts over the loudspeakers. Posters of Farrah Fawcett hang in every booth. I can't help noticing there are pretty girls with tight shirts and short shorts everywhere. I feel kind of hopped-up and crazy. My hands are tingling and the hair on the back of my neck is standing up. The smell of French fries and cotton candy makes my mouth water. I wish we had more money.

We walk along past freak-show booths with everything from bearded ladies to a headless nurse, from a girl with the body of a snake to a wild man, and even a cow with eight legs—four regular and four on its back. The sign shows the cow running normally, then flipping on its back and running with its other set of legs.

"I'd like to see that," Cid says.

"It's just a fake," I tell her. Dad would have said the same thing. He knew all about these things because he used to work for a carnival when he was young. He told us there are tricks to winning, and if you know them, you can beat the carnies at their own game. He was especially good at shooting the red out of the star. He won us all kinds of huge stuffed animals that way, which made the carnies furious.

After about half an hour of searching, we finally find the booth with the signs. It's sandwiched among a bunch of other stalls selling horse tack, brushes, hoof-picks, and treatments of every kind. A woman with a face as hard as a fist is hunched over a table, carefully burning someone's name into a thick strip of dark wood.

"How much for a sign?" I ask.

The woman doesn't look up from her work. "For what name?"

"Smokey. It's our pony."

"Ten dollars."

We look at each other in dismay. We only have six dollars, all told. "I have six."

The woman finally looks up at me. "It's ten dollars."

I push Queenie forward and give her a pinch. "But it's for my little sister. She broke her collarbone and just got her cast off today. She's been waiting for months to buy a sign from you."

I nudge Queenie, and she looks at the woman with her most mournful face. The woman stares at us, then holds up a smallish sign. "You can have something like this for six."

We look at each other, then tell the woman OK. I spell *Smokey* for her twice so she won't make a mistake.

"Come back in an hour. I'll have it ready."

We wander through the fair. Even though we don't have any more money, we enjoy looking at all the people and games and rides. Despite what I told her before, Cid still wants to see the cow with eight legs.

I search my pockets for change and find just enough to get one ticket. Queenie and I wait for ages at the bottom of the stairs. Cid finally comes out.

"It's not a fake. It's real. It has eight legs. Four regular and four more out its back. The man said it was born that way. I guess the mother was supposed to have twins and somehow they grew together. It's really creepy looking."

"Did it flip over and run on its back like in the picture?" Queenie asks.

Cid shakes her head. "Nah. That's just somebody's stupid idea to get people to come in to see it. The legs just flop around. They're useless."

We discuss the cow as we walk back to the booth for our sign. The woman has it ready and waiting for us. It's a small wooden plaque with SMOKEY written in neat letters. We let Queenie carry it, seeing as it was her idea all those weeks ago when she got hurt. We wander around the fair until we've seen all the animals and displays.

"Let's go to the barn and put the sign up," I say.

Cid groans. "I want to stay a bit longer."

"Well, you can stay. But Queenie and I want to go put the sign up."

Cid folds her arms across her chest. "Fine!"

That's when I notice a girl from my school looking at the horse tack. It's Cheryl Hanson, the prettiest girl I've ever seen. She lives in one of the big houses over in the rich neighborhood. She doesn't even know I exist.

"OK, we can stay a bit longer," I say.

Cid gives me a strange look. She opens her mouth to start in on me.

"We can stay a bit longer," I say again. "Why don't you two go look around. I'm going to look at some stuff by myself."

"But Ma said to stick together," Cid says.

"It's for Christmas," I lie. "I want to look at things for you and Queenie for Christmas."

This seems to work. Cid grabs Queenie by the hand and walks over to one of the rides. I move over to the booth where Cheryl is standing and pretend to look at the bridles. She is wearing a tie-dyed halter top, cutoff jean shorts, and clogs. I can smell her perfume and the scent of her long blond hair. My mind is spinning, trying to think of something to say. I imagine all sorts of things, like asking her out for a soda, or telling her we have a horse, or something.

While I'm thinking like this, this big jock named Tyler Long appears and puts his arm around her. He kisses her on the lips and drags her off to one of the rides, and I'm left standing there like a stupid jerk, looking at bridles I can't even afford. I know I can't compete with Tyler Long. He's rich and good-looking like John Travolta. He wears Levi's and puka beads. All the girls are crazy for him. He's in high school. He even drives.

I work my way over to where Cid and Queenie are standing. "OK, let's go."

"But we've only been here a minute," Cid protests.

"Well, I'm ready to go!" I snap.

Cid snarls back at me. "OK! You don't have to be so angry about it!"

She's right. But I can't help it. If only Cheryl had noticed me standing there, maybe things would be different. If only she had a chance to talk to me, maybe she would like me. If only . . .

The walk to the barn takes twice as long as usual because the fairgrounds are clear across town in the opposite direction. When we get there, Smokey is waiting. Cid and Queenie groom him while I attach the sign to his stall with a piece of old wire.

"It looks great," Queenie says when I've finished.

I have to admit, it does look good. We all stand admiring the sign, and somehow I forget about Cheryl Hanson and how mad I was.

"Come on. Let's go for a ride."

Summer is really over now and I'm stuck behind a desk again. I'm in eighth grade though I'm supposed to be in seventh. Ma said it would give me a challenge to skip a grade. But the only challenge I'm facing is being the youngest kid in the class. I may get good marks, but I don't like school, no matter what grade they put me in. I decided years ago that school isn't about learning—it's more like crowd control. They can't teach you anything really interesting, because they're too busy making sure the kids don't freak out and wreck stuff. I would hate school entirely, except for the fact that Cheryl Hanson is in two of my classes. And then I remember the fair and my blown attempt at meeting her. I've never had any luck talking to girls. For me, talking to girls is like trying to catch a knife by the handle. It's dangerous and kind of stupid. Mostly you just cut yourself to pieces and wonder why you try to do it at all. But sometimes, when things are just right, you can make it work, and when you do, it's the greatest feeling in the world.

As I'm sitting there, I realize I'll never have the guts to talk to Cheryl. It's not just because I'm younger, either. It's because my family is poor and everyone knows it. What girl wants to go out with a poor kid whose socks never match and who wears Toughskins from Sears instead of Levi's? Probably none. Ma tries, but she can't afford to buy us new clothes all the time, if at all. Not that I'd want to wear bell-bottoms anyway, because they look so stupid. But I would like a pair of painter pants, or even a pair of tan cords.

The teacher drones on and on. I watch the kid next to me tracing around the Adidas logo on his sneakers with a pen. Around and around and around. I swear the clock is ticking backward. I'm about ready to scream when the bell finally rings.

Outside the kids are running and hollering, thankful to be set free. Orange and red leaves swirl everywhere, and the schoolyard glows with a honey-colored light. I see Cid talking with some friends on the steps of the high school, so I leave her alone and go to look for Queenie at her school. I'm just about across the street when I notice a group of guys around Queenie. I can't tell what they're doing at first, but then it dawns on me that they're making fun of her for the way she goes off dancing sometimes.

The first kid doesn't even see me as my fist hits him in the side of the head and sends him flying. I manage to get in some good punches before the other guys jump on me. They punch and kick me and I punch and kick back, but there are just too many of them. Someone hits me in the back with something—maybe a piece of wood—and I fall to the ground. They're kicking and kicking me and I'm just trying to protect my face and ears. Through all the punching and yelling, I can hear a girl screaming, and suddenly I realize it's Cid. She's hollering and swinging her book bag like a medieval knight swinging a mace.

"Get away from him! Get away from him!"

I'm thankful that she wants to help, but all I can think about now is how this is going to look to the rest of the kids. Cid manages to scatter the fighters, because even the worst guy in the world hesitates before hitting a girl. One guy spits at her as he's running away, and Cid spits right back, then helps me to my feet. Queenie stands there, her hands covering her eyes, until the punks are gone. I can taste my own blood on my lips, and my head is splitting. Cid frets over me but I brush her hands away.

"I'm OK."

"They would have killed you."

"You should have stayed out of it."

"Look at your eye. . . ."

"I said I'm OK!"

Cid turns her back on me, and I know she's furious. That's when I notice Cheryl Hanson looking at me from the sidewalk. She stands there hugging her books to her chest and staring at me with those huge blue eyes. I turn away because she's the last person I want to see after getting my ass kicked.

"Come on, let's just go to the barn and see Smokey," I say, trying to forget the whole deal. I put my hand on Queenie's shoulder, and she looks up at me with admiration—and a little bit of worry, I think.

We walk to the barn in silence. Cid is fuming. I don't blame her, but I just can't be grateful right now. A boy shouldn't need his sister to fight his fights. It should be the other way around, which was my intention when I started this mess in the first place. Now my head feels like a cracked egg and my ribs hurt something terrible, not to mention my bruised ego. I know my lip is split, because I can still taste blood. It's going to take a long time to heal.

When we get to the barn, I let Cid and Queenie

groom Smokey. This time I'm the one sitting on the concrete feed trough. I inspect my eye in the reflection from an old silver pail. The eye is purple like an eggplant and swollen half shut. Ma's going to go crazy when she sees this. I walk over to the hose and run cold water over my face. The water stings my eye, but I know the cold will help.

"How did you get tangled up with those guys, anyway?" I finally ask, turning my good eye toward Queenie.

Queenie looks at me over Smokey's back. She shrugs and continues to brush him. I walk back and sit down on the trough again. Cid glances at me and our eyes meet.

"Thanks," I say.

Cid nods, her face sober.

"I mean it. You saved my life."

"Wasn't she cool?" Queenie pipes up. "Swinging her books like that!" She mimics Cid, swinging the brush in wild circles over her head by the end of its leather strap.

"She thinks she's Obi-Wan Kenobi," I scoff.

Cid bursts out laughing and then we all start to laugh. It *was* kind of funny.

. . .

But Ma doesn't think so. She starts yelling the second I walk through the door.

"Oh, my God, what happened to you? Who did this? They won't be so brave if I go to see them!"

Great. That's the last thing I need. My sister *and* my mom fighting battles for me. As if I'm not embarrassed enough as it is. I just stand there and let Ma yell for a while. I don't even try to explain anything at this point, because I know I won't get a word in edgewise. This may sound like an awful situation, but Ma yells when she's scared or when something doesn't make sense, which happens all the time around our house. She isn't really mad at me. She's just worried, I guess. I just wish she wouldn't worry so much.

After a long stretch of worrying, Ma fusses and clucks over my eye, pressing a bag of frozen peas covered in a tea towel against my face. I'm just glad that we agreed we wouldn't tell Ma the truth about Queenie being picked on, because that would worry her even more. She is already threatening to go down to the schoolyard as it is. I tell her a whopper about fighting over some girl. I know she will respect that. I console myself with the fact that it's not a total lie. Queenie's a girl, isn't she?

I've decided my history teacher, Mrs. Malanus, has it in for me. She never lays off for a second, always bugging me for answers to this and that. She thinks I'm some kind of genius or something, because she calls on me whenever one of the other kids can't answer a question. This is the second-best way to get beat up at school. Even if I do know the answer, which I usually do, I don't like showing off. So sometimes I just shrug and pretend I don't know, like when she asked me to name all the different architectural styles of columns or explain what flying buttresses are and what they're used for, or some other thing like that.

I can't help it if I know things. I like to read and that's what I do at lunch instead of sitting with the other kids in the cafeteria. I hate the cafeteria. I hate seeing all those mouths eating. Rows and rows of mouths opening and closing and chewing. It makes me feel kind of crazy. Besides, I never have a lunch to bring and I sure don't want to waste my paper route money buying food, so I just skip lunch altogether and read. I like history, and I like reading about things like how buildings are made and why. But I don't want this fact broadcast all over the school.

Mrs. Malanus won't quit today, though. She puts a map of Quebec on the board and starts asking questions about *coureurs de bois*. She pronounces it "*koor-ee-ur de bwaz*." Now I know all about how the *coureurs de bois* lived and how they trapped beaver and things to trade with the Métis. I even know how to pronounce the name correctly. They were woodsmen, and they're an important part of Canadian history. I would like to live like a *coureur de bois,* riding Smokey through the wilderness, smoking tobacco, trading furs for weapons, building shelters in the snow if I needed to, and maybe even shooting a few people who poached from my traps—but I wouldn't tell anyone in school about that.

"Who were the *koor-ee-ur de bwaz?*" Mrs. Malanus asks the class.

Silence.

"Maria?"

Maria shrugs.

"Jim?"

Jim does the same.

"Anybody?"

I hide behind my history text, pretending to disappear. I just know she's going to call on me next.

"Nathaniel?"

I pretend I don't hear and keep hiding.

"Nathaniel?"

There is an awful silence. I want to just shrug like the other kids and get out of it, but she won't let up. I can hear all the kids creaking around in their seats to look at me. I glance over my shoulder and find Cheryl Hanson staring back at me from her seat at the back of the class. Her long blond hair curls and flows over her shoulders. Her mouth is red like a cherry, and she's wearing a tight pink sweater. I can feel her big blue eyes burning right through me, and suddenly we are the only two people in the room. But we're not in the room anymore. We're in a beautiful field full of wildflowers, stretched out next to each other on a blanket with Smokey quietly grazing nearby. Cheryl's hair tumbles all around my face as I lean toward her and press my lips against her mouth—

"Nathaniel!" the teacher screams, and I nearly hit the ceiling.

The other kids burst out laughing, and I can feel my face burning red with embarrassment.

Just then, the bell rings and I am saved for another day. I slam my books shut and run out of the class. I'm nearly out the school door when I feel a tug on my shirt—I think Mrs. Malanus must have caught me. I turn around, ready to defend myself so I won't get a detention, and find Cheryl Hanson's beautiful blue eyes smiling back at me.

"Hey, going to a fire?"

I feel my face turning red again. I mumble into my shirt, hoping she won't notice. "Oh, no, just trying to get away from that cow Malanus."

"She really had it in for you today," Cheryl says. Her even white teeth gleam like pearls.

"Yeah. She never lays off."

"I thought it was brave the way you stuck up for your sister the other day."

"Yeah, sure. Except I got my head kicked in by those guys."

"I thought it was really brave," she says again. "Your sister . . . she does that funny thing. . . ."

"It doesn't mean anything," I blurt out. "She's always done it. She's just too smart for her own good. She gets caught up in her thoughts. She's not deficient or anything. . . ."

Cheryl just looks at me. I think she's going to give me the brushoff. And then she says something that I never could have hoped for.

"Walk me home?"

She says this as easily as though she were asking me something simple and meaningless, like, did I have my homework done, or did I know what page we were supposed to read for history. She bumps her shoulder playfully against mine. I stand there just staring at her, because I can't believe my ears. Suddenly I can't speak at all. Did she really ask me to walk her home? We don't even live in the same neighborhood. We don't even live on the same planet, for that matter. Her parents are rich and own a huge house in the nice part of town. I'm sure they would be furious if they knew I was anywhere near their daughter. But I can't believe my luck, and so I just nod and walk beside her.

I've dreamed of this moment for so long, yet somehow I can't think of one word to say. I don't even ask if I can carry her books, because I don't want to make any assumptions. I look over at her and she is holding her books against her chest, the sun shining and dancing on her long blond curls. I know the sun shines on everybody, but with Cheryl it's different. It's as though the light is coming from somewhere inside her—like she *is* the sun, radiating warmth and beauty all over the world. I would love to run my hand through her hair and smell the sunshine in it. I would love to slip my hand in hers and feel the pulse of her next to me. I'm thinking this way when suddenly my dreams are burst by a loud voice.

"Hey, Cheryl!"

It's Tyler Long, looking every bit the jock in his tight jeans and his football jersey. You can bet he never had a paper route or had to patch holes in his pants. He's never done anything to me, but I hate him anyway. I guess I should be glad he doesn't push me around or try to embarrass me in public. Yet, for some reason, it seems worse that he just ignores me. He's too old for Cheryl, I tell myself, even though she's one of those girls who always seem to be with older, more successful guys. He pulls up in his parents' shiny yellow convertible and opens the passenger side door like I'm not even there.

"Come on. Get in."

Cheryl gives me a look like she's sorry and then trots over to Tyler's car. "See you tomorrow," she says sweetly, and waves before she disappears around the corner. *Just like the daffodils,* I can't help thinking. One day they appear out of nowhere, and before you know it, they're gone. Like everything in my life.

I think about Dad, and suddenly I'm feeling so angry and stupid that I decide to skip delivering my papers until later. I just have to see Smokey. I run up the street toward the road to the barn and see Cid and Queenie already at the top of the hill. "Hey!" I yell, waving madly. They keep walking. I guess they don't hear me. "Hey!" I yell again, then start running up the hill. I finally catch up to them and tug on Cid's coat. "Are you guys deaf?"

"Ma told us to never turn around when someone yells like that," Cid says disdainfully.

"It's different when it's your brother."

"How are we supposed to know the difference unless we turn around?" she says smugly.

She's got a point.

"Never mind."

We walk up the hill in silence, Queenie doing her little dance the whole way to the barn. I don't try to stop her, because my mind is back with Cheryl Hanson, walking along the sidewalk to the good side of town.

Smokey whinnies happily when he sees us. The barn smells sweet and earthy. The sunlight filters through the slats of the walls, filling the barn with a dusky gold light. Smokey snorts contentedly in his stall, munching loudly on the last bits of hay in his trough. We take our time brushing him and picking out his feet before tacking him up and taking him to the field for a gallop.

As usual, Cid wants to ride first. Normally I would argue with her—just for general purposes—but I can't bring myself to do it today. Cid jumps on Smokey's back, reins him to the right, and canters full out along the length of the fence. Smokey whirls like a pinwheel, his mane and tail flying, his hooves beating a quick rhythm against the ground. They dip out of sight below a small hill, then reappear along a crest in the field. They ride into the glowing ball of the sun, fusing with the orange light.

I can't see them anymore, but I can feel Smokey as warm and as real as though I'm on him, and I forget about everything else. I forget about Mrs. Malanus and Tyler Long and even Cheryl Hanson. I forget about Clem's ghost. I forget that we're poor and have to steal moldy old hay. I forget about Dad leaving us. I forget about it all.

I turn to look at Queenie. She is smiling and squinting into the sunlight. Her face is bathed in orange, the round ball of the sun reflected in her eyes. I feel so close to her right now. I know she understands the way I feel. I know she feels the same way, too.

a wild ride

We wake up one morning to find the world buried under a ton of snow. It covers the rooftops and lawns like a heavy white comforter. It's early November, and I can't ever remember the snow coming so soon. But the best part of all is that it's Saturday and we don't have to go to school.

"We can try out my new sled," I tell Queenie as she struggles with her boots in the hallway.

Ma gave me the sled for my birthday. It's red plastic and doesn't have a scratch on it. I've kept it in my room for weeks, waiting for the snow.

"You mean, hitch Smokey to it?"

"Yeah. It'll be great. We'll make a harness out of twine and run it back to the sled. Then we'll cluck like this"—I make a clucking sound with my tongue—"and Smokey will trot along, as pretty as you please. He's strong enough to pull all of us at once, but the sled can only carry two comfortably."

"Who gets to go first?" Cid asks.

"It's my sled, so you two will have to fight it out to see who gets to ride with me. Pick a number."

"Three!" Queenie says right away.

"Forget it!" Cid protests. "I don't trust you guys."

"Fine. We'll draw straws. We'll do it when we get to the barn."

We call out good-bye to Ma, who's holed up in her room reading some Agatha Christie murder mystery for the umpteenth time. She loves to read so much that she's read every book at the public library at least three times.

"Watch the traffic. The roads will be slippery!" she says.

"We will."

"Queenie, you button up your coat and wear a hat—I don't care how itchy you get!"

"Yes, Ma."

"And mind you get home before dark! I don't want to be worrying about you kids wandering home at all hours!"

Ma is still calling out orders as we slip through the door and bump my new red sled down the stairs into the snow.

"How'll we attach Smokey to it?" Cid asks.

"We're going to make a harness out of twine," Queenie says with authority, as though it were her idea.

"Won't it cut into his chest? Won't it just break?"

"Nat's going to make a breastplate using sheepskin or something. It'll be soft and strong, and Smokey will trot along as pretty as you please."

Queenie repeats the words I said earlier like they're gospel. That's what I love about her. She's always right onboard. I don't even have to explain things to her the way I do to Cid. She just innocently goes along with pretty much everything I suggest. Sometimes I wish I could be innocent like that again.

"Where are we supposed to get the sheepskin?" Cid asks.

"I've got some ideas," I tell her, just to stop the questions from spoiling the magic of the new snow.

Our boots clump loudly through the streets, the steam from our breath curling around our faces and resting in white crystals on our caps and eyelashes. It's hard going up the hill to the barn, with cars skidding and sliding on the icy streets. I'm tempted to hitch a ride on a car's back bumper but know I'd never hear the end of it if Cid or Queenie fell off and got hurt. So we stomp along, talking excitedly about the possibilities once we teach Smokey to pull the sled.

The Gorilla is at the barn when we arrive, brushing his Morgan colt, the colt in cross-ties in the aisle. We ignore him, save for a mumbled greeting when we first enter the barn, but he insists on talking to us all the same.

"You kids been going through my tack box? I'm missing some brushes and things."

"We have our own tack," I answer in a way that Ma would call snotty, but I can't help it. He has no right to accuse us of anything—even though I did use his bleach.

"Well, I don't want to find out you've been using my things."

"We have no reason to use your things. We have our own—just like I said two seconds ago."

The Gorilla gives me a look that says, *Watch it, kid,* but I don't even flinch. He can't tell us what to do now that Smokey is gelded. I lean my sled against the wall, and the Gorilla and I stare at each other like we're in a showdown in some Western. Queenie starts to dance. I guess all this anger makes her feel nervous.

"What's wrong with your sister?" the Gorilla asks, jerking his head in Queenie's direction.

"There's nothing wrong with her. You just mind your own business."

"Then why is she always dancing around like some kind of mental patient?"

"I said there's nothing wrong with her."

I fold my arms over my chest and we stare at each other some more, until he finally looks away and I know I've won.

"I was just asking," he says, turning his back on me.

I grab Queenie and pull her into Smokey's stall. I know it's not her fault that she dances. I just wish she wouldn't do it in public. I wish she would grow out of it. I can't even remember when she started dancing. She's always done it in some form or another, I guess. Even so, the Gorilla has no right saying the things he said. Sometimes I wish I could mutate into a giant green monster like the Incredible Hulk. People might be a little more careful about what they say to me then.

I hand Queenie a pitchfork, and we work at cleaning Smokey's stall. Then all three of us groom him very carefully and slowly, waiting for the Gorilla to put his colt away and get out. I don't want him seeing us hitching Smokey to the sled. He'd just have some comment about what a bad idea it was and how stupid we were, or something.

My arm is sore from brushing by the time the Gorilla finally leaves. We wasted half the morning waiting for him to pack up and go. As soon as we hear his truck leave, I walk down the aisle and open his tack box.

"What are you doing?" Cid asks.

"Getting something."

"If you take his stuff, he'll kill us."

"He won't know. Besides, he can afford to replace it. And if he's going to accuse us of stealing anyway, we may as well make the most of it."

I pull an expensive leather halter from the box and eye the sheepskin noseband with certain intention. "This will do just fine."

"Nathaniel, don't you dare!" Cid says. "It's bad enough we're stealing hay!"

"We'll put it back. Do you want the rope to hurt Smokey?"

Cid shakes her head in disbelief. Queenie watches with interest.

"We'll just use it until I can get enough money from my paper route to buy the proper thing. Christmas is coming, so I should have some money soon."

Queenie and I gather binder twine, then braid several pieces together as thick and flat as we can, designing it harnesslike to fit across Smokey's chest and along his sides. We even braid long reins and a piece to go behind his withers to hold the harness in place. Before we attach the two pieces, I work the borrowed sheepskin noseband from the Gorilla's halter along the length of the braid and to the center of the rope harness. Then I tie it all together and hold it up.

"Looks pretty good," Queenie says approvingly.

I don't even look at Cid for an opinion, because I know she thinks I'm a creep for taking the sheepskin. I'm sure she's scared we'll get caught, and I am, too—just a little—but I don't want to hurt Smokey with the rope. So the borrowing can't be helped.

"Let's try it out."

I grab the sled, and we lead Smokey from his stall into the field. He snorts and blows at the snow, tossing his head with excitement at the transformed landscape. The snow makes the tufts of grass in the field look like cupcakes. The sun is so bright, it mixes the field and sky and everything in shades of blue. Queenie holds Smokey's head while I tie the twine reins to his halter. Then I slip the harness over his head, tying the ropes to the front of the sled. Smokey eyes me suspiciously as I secure the final knot.

"We'd best lead him around a bit to get him used to it," I tell Queenie.

Queenie leads Smokey around, the sled sliding behind him. Smokey pins his ears back, then lunges forward, setting Queenie off balance. I grab the halter and hold him steady. We lead him around and around, but Smokey's ears stay pinned to his head.

"He'll be OK once he understands what the sled is for," I say.

"Let me get on," Cid says.

We let Cid get on, Queenie and I holding either side of Smokey's halter. Cid takes the reins in her mittened hands.

"Come on, Queenie, get on. We'll go for a ride."

But before Queenie can take a step toward the sled, Smokey rears forward and bolts, sending me and Queenie flying. Cid pulls on the reins with all her might, but Smokey doesn't pay any mind. He gallops full speed toward the fence, Cid sliding and tipping on the sled behind him.

"Hang on!" I yell.

But it's no use. Smokey breaks to the left, sending Cid tumbling off the sled like a bag of old clothes. Smokey gallops and kicks furiously, the sled dipping and flapping angrily behind him.

"He's going to hurt himself!" Queenie yells, as Smokey bucks and kicks toward the fence.

At last the rope can hold no more and the sled breaks free, sliding to a stop at the bottom of the hill. It takes us nearly half an hour to catch Smokey and calm him down. And the sled sure doesn't look new anymore. There are a bunch of dents at the front. I wouldn't want Ma to see that. She'd think I didn't appreciate the sled. But I do. It's just going to take Smokey a bit to get used to it.

"If at first you don't succeed . . ." I say, moving slowly behind Smokey while the girls hold his head and soothe him with gentle talk.

"He'll never get used to it, Nathaniel," Cid says.

"We'll see. Rome wasn't built in a day."

"Rome wasn't a frightened pony."

"He can do it. We just have to be patient."

When I have the sled tied on properly, I tell Cid to get on again—only this time, more to the back of the sled.

"Forget it! I'm not stupid."

"We need the weight," I explain. "I'm getting on, too. The weight will slow Smokey down so he can't run as fast."

I get Queenie to hold Smokey's head while I carefully lower myself onto the front of the sled. Smokey pins his ears back, just like before, but this time when he lunges forward, he can only pull us along at a walk. I cluck with my tongue and gently snap the twine reins against his back. Smokey swings his head from side to side, lifting his hooves like a Paso Fino stallion through the snow.

"He's doing it!" Queenie yells.

I rein Smokey to the deeper snow so the sled can slide more easily. I can feel the grass cupcakes bumping along the bottom of the sled. Cid is holding me tight around the waist.

"This is so fun!" she laughs.

I give the reins another little shake, and Smokey quickens his pace to a trot. We move nicely up the hill, back toward Queenie and the barn.

"Can I go next?" Queenie asks.

Cid doesn't argue as she stands up from the sled and moves to hold Smokey's halter so that Queenie can get on. Queenie sits carefully behind me, holding me around the waist the way Cid did. I cluck my tongue and snap the reins against Smokey's back. "Hold on!"

Smokey moves forward more gracefully now, his bright eyes shining, his mane tossing and waving. I cluck again and Smokey breaks into a trot. Queenie and I glide smoothly along the length of the fence, the cold air biting our cheeks and noses, the sound of the sled swishing across the snow.

"I told you it would work!"

Queenie hugs me, pressing her face against my back as we circle around and around the field. When it seems like Smokey is used to the idea of the sled, I get off and let Cid take the reins. She trots Smokey over and across the field, Queenie sitting proudly behind her. We go on like this for most of the afternoon, until the sun starts to sink low in the sky.

Inside the barn, we carefully groom Smokey and

towel the sweat from his coat so he won't catch a chill. We cover him with one of Ma's old wool blankets, fastening it at the chest and under the belly with clothes pegs from the laundry basket. I fill Smokey's trough with hay from the loft. So far no one has even noticed that we've been taking it. I guess I would feel guiltier if they were around more or keeping an eye on things, but they aren't. Besides, we feed Ted Henry's horse all the time, too, so he can consider the hay and straw we take as payment of sorts. I fluff straw around the stall, then pour fresh water into Smokey's bucket. Then I return the sheepskin noseband to its rightful place. When we leave, Smokey is munching happily on his hay, glad to be back in his stall.

"You were right, Nat," Queenie says. "He did go just as pretty as you please."

For some reason this makes Cid and me laugh. I run ahead to the street and slide with my boots on the packed snow. Cid and Queenie follow, and then we're all sliding and laughing down the hill toward home.

christmas magic

I'm jolted awake first thing in the morning by the sound of Ma's angry voice. I think she's yelling at me, so I snap on my little bedside lamp to see what I'm in trouble for now. Then I realize she's on the phone. Ma's voice gets really high and it cracks when she's particularly mad. I can't imagine who could possibly deserve the kind of tongue-lashing Ma's handing out right now, so I lay in bed listening. *Better them than me* is all I can think.

While I'm listening, I blow out my breath and watch it steam in the air. It's only four days before Christmas, and the house is colder than a dead star. Ma keeps the house so cold, the pipes freeze from time to time. She says she keeps the heat low to save money. I don't see this as any kind of savings because it means that Ma has to call the plumber when things go wrong. He replaces a few things, then tells her to turn up the heat in the house. Sometimes she even lets the taps run at a trickle to keep the lines open. This must cost money, too, I think.

I wish she would just turn the heat up in the first place, because I have to sleep in my long johns to keep from freezing like the pipes. I almost never go to bed without socks. In the morning I usually jump straight into my jeans without taking off my long johns, because it's too cold in the house to bear the idea of undressing all the way.

All of a sudden my little lamp goes out. I hear the phone slam down in the cradle and Ma swearing a blue streak. This makes me sit straight up in bed, because that's something Ma never does unless she's ready to kill somebody. But she's swearing now—like the best of them. I sit there in the dark, straining to hear. Then Cid bursts into my room.

"What's going on?"

Queenie is right behind her, padding along in her fuzzy pink pajamas, the ones with the feet cut off because she grew too tall for them.

"I don't know. But Ma was yelling just a second ago and now the lights are out."

I whip the covers off and push my sock feet into a pair of hand-knit slippers that are missing the pompoms and whose soles have been patched so many times you can't tell what the original color must have been. I pull on some sweatpants and a sweatshirt and go out into the hall to hear better. That's when I realize that Ma is crying. I rush down the stairs without even thinking, Queenie and Cid right behind me.

"Ma! What's going on?"

"Oh, those horrible people!"

"What horrible people, Ma?"

"The electric company. They turned off the power because I'm late paying the bill. I told them Friday at the latest, but they wouldn't listen."

This makes me more than just a little scared. We've been hungry before and we've had to make do with old clothes, but we've never had to face anything like this. And only four days before Christmas. Suddenly I hate my dad more than ever. How could he go and leave us to freeze with no electricity, while he and his new family eat steaks and things? I'm not sure about the steaks, but that's the first thing that comes to my mind and it makes me furious.

"That can't be legal, Ma, to shut off the power." This is all I can think to say. To my surprise, she doesn't treat me like an idiot.

"No, it's not legal. And I'm going to do something about it."

I look over at Queenie and Cid, who haven't said a word. I can tell they're scared, too, because they've never seen Ma like this before, either. Ma tears the phone book open to the government pages, flipping angrily through until she finds the number she wants. She dials the numbers so hard, she has to redial twice just to get it right.

"May I speak with the mayor, please?"

I look at Cid and Queenie as though to say, *Do you believe Ma's guts?* Then I shrug because I have no idea what's coming next.

"I have to speak to her. It's very important."

There's a long pause.

"Then I'd like to leave her a message. I'm a single mother struggling to survive with three children. I've always tried to pay my bills on time. I try to do my best, but the electric company won't wait for one more day and decided to just cut us off. My children are here in the dark, and we can't even put the kettle on the stove for a cup of tea. This is a disgrace, and I want something done about it immediately."

After bending the secretary's ear, Ma leaves her name and number and hangs up. She folds her arms across her chest and disappears into her room, leaving us standing in the hallway by the phone with no explanation as to what's going to happen.

"We can light the fire," I tell Queenie and Cid to make them feel better. "It's kind of exciting with no electricity. Just like *Little House on the Prairie*."

"Are we going to freeze to death?" Queenie asks.

I look at her in shock and then laugh to let her know that everything will be all right. But honestly, this whole thing has me really scared. I don't know if the mayor will call us back, and even if she does, what good can she do? She won't pay our bills or make Dad come home and take care of us. I feel sorry for Ma, having to call the mayor and embarrass herself like that. I feel sorry for the whole lot of us.

"Get some newspaper from the garbage," I order Queenie, to keep her busy. "Go get the matches in the kitchen drawer," I order Cid for the same reason.

They don't argue, but just obediently get what I

asked for, which means they're depending on me to get them through this. I hate being in this position, but I do it all the same because somebody has to take charge.

I don't even have a chance to light the newspaper in the fireplace when the lights snap on. The phone rings as this happens, and I shake out the match and rush to answer it. I can't believe my ears when I hear it's the mayor. I yell for Ma to come to the phone, and she appears like summer lightning, snatching the phone from my outstretched hand.

"Hello . . ."

I think Ma is as surprised as the rest of us that the mayor actually called back. We all stand there listening. There's a long pause, and I'm desperate to know what's being said.

"Yes. Yes. Well, thank you very much. I appreciate this very much." Ma returns the phone to its cradle, then leans her chin on one hand and just stares off into space.

"What'd she say, Ma?" the three of us ask together.

"She called the power company and told them to turn on the electricity and not to turn it off again, no matter how late we are paying the bill."

Cid, Queenie, and I exchange astonished looks. "That was nice of her," I finally say.

"Yes, it was. She's a woman with a family of her own. I knew she'd understand." Ma suddenly looks at her watch in alarm. "Good lord, you kids are going to be late for school!"

I knew the time had been ticking away, but I wasn't going to get dressed and go to school and leave Ma alone in the dark. I open my mouth to explain this, but Ma cuts me short.

"You can stay home today. You won't make it in time for the bell, and none of you has had anything to eat yet. Just make sure you catch up on your homework tomorrow. And keep an eye on the fire if you light it."

Ma gets ready for work faster than I've ever seen her do. She looks like Bob Cratchit from *A Christmas Carol* with her long hand-knitted scarf wound around and around her neck and her gloves with the finger-tips cut out so she can wear them while she's typing at the office. She needs them like that because her office is almost always cold. Her boss, Mr. McKinley, is a fossil from the Dark Ages with his dingy wallpaper and his junky old machinery that he refuses to replace. Luke Skywalker is flying all over the universe, and Ma is still typing on a manual typewriter. All the other secretaries who work for other lawyers in town get to use those new IBM electric typewriters. Ma says they work with a little ball that whizzes around to type the letters, instead of individual arms like the old-style typewriters. She says the other secretaries write such nice, neat letters because they have all the right equipment, but old bachelor McKinley doesn't give a darn about things like that.

Still, despite the old-fashioned equipment and peeling wallpaper, working for Mr. McKinley has its advantages. He's so old, he barely has any clients left, and he does all the title-searching himself because he doesn't trust Ma to do it, which means he's out of the office a lot. There's not enough work for Ma to do, so she occupies her time knitting mittens and things for us, or practicing her recorder, or just putting her feet up against the space heater and singing Christmas carols if she wants to. I've seen her do that. It's the best job for Ma, seeing as she doesn't have a lot of work experience. She actually likes it, even though she has to be there at the crack of dawn and doesn't come home until long after we're home from school. And McKinley is as honest as the day is long, Ma says. She told us that he once got a quarter from a machine that he shouldn't have, so he sealed it in an envelope and sent it back to the company with an explanation. I thought he was an idiot to do it, but Ma said it's just because his conscience won't let him keep so much as a quarter that isn't his. We started calling him Abe Lincoln after that, because I heard once that Lincoln walked miles to return a penny to a man who had dropped it. This makes Ma laugh, but she made us promise we would never say it outside of the house.

Ma calls out a few last-minute instructions before shutting the door and tramping down the snowy stairs to the sidewalk. We wave from the window, watching her until she's just a dark shape against the white snow at the top of the street, then shriek and jump around the living room like monkeys. It's not that we're glad Ma isn't here. It's just unusual for all three of us to be allowed to stay home on a school day with no one being sick or anything.

When we are finished acting wild, I work on getting the fire started. We haven't got any kindling, so I pull strips of bark from the logs instead. While I'm doing this, Queenie and Cid make toast and coffee with the few heels of bread left in the bread drawer.

We haven't got a toaster. We put the bread under the grill of the stove.

"You watch those heels don't burn!" I call out. This makes me laugh because more than once I've melted the soles of my shoes putting them too close to the fire.

We only have a bit of butter, so Cid carefully greases the toasted heels, then slices them into little cubes. She puts them in the bowls of coffee, the butter floating in hundreds of tiny circles on the surface. Then she piles the toast cubes with spoonfuls of sugar until they sink like small square ships to the bottom of the bowl. This is what we eat when Ma isn't around to cook, and it suits us just fine. The fire is crackling merrily and I couldn't be happier, sitting there with my two sisters, indulging ourselves with a hot toast-and-coffee breakfast. We eat in silence for a bit, enjoying the warm comfort of the flames.

"Do you think the electric company will listen to the mayor?" Queenie asks thoughtfully.

"Sure they will. They haven't got a choice." I slurp loudly at my coffee because Ma isn't around to stop me.

"Will they go to jail if they do it again?"

"I don't think so." I answer seriously, but secretly

I'm thrilled at the idea of all the electric company people rotting in jail for turning off our power.

"Do you think Ma will let us get a tree?" Queenie asks, changing the subject abruptly, as only she can.

"A Christmas tree?"

"Yeah. A nice big one like we had in the stone house."

This is the way we measure time in my family. Not in years, like most people, but by houses that we've lived in.

"We never even had a tree like that in the yellow house," Cid pipes up. "We could never afford a tree like that again."

"Who says?" I challenge her, just because I feel like it today.

"We can't even pay our electric bill, Nathaniel. How is Ma going to afford any tree at all, let alone one as big as that?"

I know she's right but I hate to admit defeat. I would use my own money to buy a tree, but I don't have more than a dollar in my cigar box right now. Besides, I want to save every cent to buy a harness strap for Smokey. I tell Queenie there's no harm in asking Ma for a tree.

We sit in front of the fire talking like this all

morning. It isn't long before Ma returns for lunch. She bangs the snow from her boots as she unwinds her scarf.

"Fire looks nice," she says cheerfully.

She's in a much better mood than when she left, so I elbow Queenie as hard as I can to let her know she should ask about the Christmas tree. It's best if Queenie asks, because Ma can't deny her anything. Queenie looks confused, then understands. She puts on her most endearing expression.

"Can we get a Christmas tree, Ma?"

Ma doesn't turn around. She picks some invisible lint off her coat for a while and doesn't answer.

"Can we get a Christmas tree, Ma?" Queenie asks again.

"We can't even pay the bills," Ma finally says in a sad voice. "I don't know what I'm supposed to buy a tree with."

Cid glares at me with that *I told you so!* look on her face.

"You could write a check," Queenie innocently persists, just as I groomed her to say.

"You can't write checks with no money in the bank. It's fraudulent," Ma says.

I jump in. "But you can put the money in when you get paid. The bank won't know. How are we supposed to have Christmas without a tree?"

This last part hangs in the air like candle smoke. We sit dumbly staring at Ma's back for what seems like the longest time, while the smoke expands and fills up the room. Ma stands with her hands in her pockets, saying nothing. Then she pulls out her checkbook, solemnly writes a check, and tears it off from the pack. She hands it to me because she thinks I'm the most responsible, I guess, or because she knows that Queenie couldn't possibly have planned this attack.

"It's all I have."

I look at the check, and it's for five dollars. I don't know what kind of tree we can buy with five dollars, but I'm so happy we got anything that I fold the check and stuff it into my pocket. "Come on, guys. We'll go get Smokey and hitch him to the sled to get the tree."

The idea of Smokey pulling the tree on the sled is so exciting, we can barely get dressed fast enough. On the way to the barn, we practically burst with anticipation, suddenly running in short fits until the cold hurts our lungs and makes us stop. We don't even practice our aim like we normally do, by throwing snowballs at traffic signs and trees, because we don't want to slow down long enough to make the snowballs.

When we reach the barn, we tumble in, stamping the snow from our boots. Smokey nickers from inside his stall, little bits of hay sticking out of his mouth. The other horses eye us curiously, picking up on our excitement.

"Put Smokey's halter and lead on," I tell Cid as I grab the pick to clean Smokey's hooves. "Give him a quick brush, Queenie. We want him to look nice."

"I brought some things," Queenie says, pulling some bits of tinsel and a handful of thin red ribbons from her coat pocket. "I've been saving these since last year. I even brought some little pinecones. I thought we could put them in his mane and tail."

"That's stupid," Cid says. "A horse should wear bells, not pinecones."

"No, it's not. It's a good idea," I tell Queenie. "Those pinecones are about the same size as bells. They just don't ring as loud." I give Queenie a wink. "You go ahead and try it out."

I take the Gorilla's noseband and work it onto the harness, while Queenie busies herself by carefully tying the little pinecones to the ends of the ribbons. When she's done this, she braids them into Smokey's mane and tail so that the cones hang down like bells. She tucks the bits of tinsel here and there through the braids, then gives Smokey's tail one last brush for good measure. She steps back when she's done, and to my surprise, it looks beautiful. Normally I shy away from this kind of thing, but Smokey looks so wonderful with Queenie's ribbons and little pinecones that my heart just soars. I put my arm around Queenie and give her a hug as she beams at her handiwork.

"It looks really good," Cid finally sniffs. "It looks like Christmas."

Maybe it's the snow on the ground or the chill in the air, but Smokey seems to know that today is special. He tosses his head and picks up his feet extra high as we parade down the street to town. The pinecones bounce and swing from his mane and tail, and everybody on the street either waves or stops to watch us go by. Even the cars slow down and little kids wave from the back seats, like we're Santa Claus or something. Cid and I wave back sometimes, but Queenie is transfixed by Smokey and the tiny pinecones.

Smokey's eyes look mischievous and bright. His coat is frosty and white, as though he sprang magically to life from a snowdrift. The steam from his muzzle curls around my hand, and I feel like the happiest person on earth.

"We oughta get him hoof black," Queenie says all of a sudden.

"That would be good," Cid agrees.

"They've got hoof paint in sparkling silver. I've seen it at the co-op," I say.

"Can we get some, Nat?" Queenie asks. "Wouldn't he look pretty with silver hooves?"

"Don't you think he'd look prettier if we painted his three black hooves black and his one white hoof silver?"

"Can we do that, Nat? That would be great."

We're so involved in this discussion that before we know it, we've reached our destination: the Towers Department Store parking lot. The trees are piled as high as a house and point every which way. There are trees leaning drunkenly against the snow fence and rejected trees scattered on the ground. The air is thick with the smell of pine. The man selling the trees looks surprised as he watches us pull up with our rig. We tie Smokey to the fence that holds the trees in, and I am happy to say that he stands nicely. Then we start the lengthy and very involved process of picking a tree that will satisfy us all with the little money that Ma gave us. It's my job to hold up the trees for Queenie and Cid's inspection. There's no sign saying how much the trees cost, so I pick up one of the smaller ones and hold it out at arm's length.

"What about this one?"

"Too skinny," Queenie says.

"What about this one?"

"Too short."

"Okay, how about this one?"

Queenie and Cid shake their heads without offering an explanation. We go on like this for a few more trees, until the man walks over.

"Can I help you kids?"

I pull the check out of my pocket and hand it to him. "What can we get for this?"

The man unfolds the check and stares at it in confusion. He looks up at us, then over at Smokey, who shakes his head impatiently. The man doesn't say a word, but folds the check and pushes it into his pocket. He walks to the back of the lot and produces a tree, slamming the trunk on the ground to show the spread of its branches. The tree is full and fresh and tall—taller than me on my tiptoes! Its branches are thick and even, with perfect little pinecones on the tips. I can't believe my eyes, because it's the nicest tree I've ever seen. It's even nicer than the one we had at the stone house. It must be worth at least fifteen or twenty dollars, but I'm not going to argue with the man. "We'll take it."

"How are you getting it home? The pony?" the man asks.

"Yes, sir. He's trained to pull. We trained him ourselves." I can't help boasting just a little.

The man quickly saws the end off the trunk to make a fresh cut, then carries the tree over to the fence for us, placing it gingerly on the sled behind Smokey. Smokey eyes the tree with suspicion, then shakes his head again.

"It's OK, mister, he won't kick," I reassure the man. "He's just never hauled a Christmas tree before."

We help the man lash the tree onto the sled with binder twine. Queenie holds Smokey's head while Cid and I check to make sure the tree is on tight.

"You kids have a merry Christmas," the man says as we lead Smokey from the lot, the tree on the sled sliding along easily.

Now we're more excited than ever because we can't believe our luck. Imagine, a tree this nice for only five dollars!

"Ma's never going to believe it," I say. "She'll be so happy when she sees the tree."

"That sure was nice of that man," Queenie says, jumping and skipping alongside the sled.

"He probably thought the check said fifty dollars," Cid scoffs.

"Maybe he was just being nice," I say. "Or maybe he was selling the trees for cheap because it's so close to Christmas. Anyway, I don't care. It's the nicest tree in town."

"What are we going to call it?" Queenie asks.

"Call what?"

"The tree. What are we going to call the tree? It has to have a name."

"How about Tannenbaum?" I offer.

"That's what we called the tree last year."

"How about Bruce the Spruce?"

"It's a fir," Cid snorts.

"Okay, genius, let's hear some suggestions."

"How about Douglas?" Cid says smugly.

"Douglas?"

"Douglas Fir."

"That's good! That's a great name!" Queenie squeals.

So we drag Douglas through town like a green patient on a red stretcher. He cooperates for the most part, but occasionally slips over a hump of snow, dipping sideways off the sidewalk and into the street. We stop Smokey when this happens, to prevent the rope of our homemade harness from running across his back legs. Smokey doesn't like when the tree comes too close. He pins his ears flat against his head.

"Watch he doesn't kick you," I tell Cid as she adjusts the sled.

The sled slides off the sidewalk almost immediately, and I'm thinking I may have to drag it myself just to save Smokey the frustration. But then I have a great idea. I tie another piece of twine to the back of the sled and walk behind like a guide, pulling the rope tight to keep the sled at the proper distance. This works beautifully and even prevents it from running too quickly down hills and hitting Smokey in the fetlocks.

As we're walking along like this, talking about how we are going to decorate the tree, big white flakes of snow start to fall all around us. They land magically on our hats and shoulders. They land on Smokey's back and his eyelashes, and they cover Douglas in a fine, white blanket.

"The tree looks beautiful just like that," Queenie muses, and I have to agree.

When we pull up to the house, Ma is already home from work and waving through the front window. She sees Smokey and rushes to the door.

"He's beautiful! Who did all the ribbons?"

This is the first time she's seen Smokey.

"Queenie did," I tell her. "Aren't they nice? You should have seen it, Ma. We had the whole town watching us as we pulled Douglas along."

"Who's Douglas?" Ma asks.

"The tree!" we all say.

"The tree? Well, Lord love you, where did you get such a nice tree?" she says, picking her way down the snowy stairs in her slippers.

"We got it at Towers," Queenie says innocently.

I can tell Ma doesn't believe us, so I explain the whole story about how I gave the man the check and how he picked the tree for us. Ma just stands there shaking her head.

"It's absolutely beautiful," she says. "Can you bring it inside? I'll have to find the tree stand in the basement. I didn't think you'd actually come home with a tree at all, certainly not one this big. . . ." She disappears into the house muttering exclamations of astonishment under her breath.

While Ma's looking for the tree stand, we hitch Smokey to the railing at the front of the house and unlash Douglas from his stretcher. The smell of tree pitch fills the air. Queenie holds the door open while Cid and I wrestle Douglas up the stairs and into the house. We dance him into the living room, careful not to bump the trunk on the carpet. Ma rushes up from the basement with the stand and places it on the carpet in front of the living-room window. We lower Douglas into the stand, and then I try to hold him straight while Cid tightens the screws and Ma and Queenie give directions either left or right. After what seems like an hour, Ma finally declares the tree fit.

"Can we decorate it now?" Queenie asks.

"Sure," Ma says, "but you'll have to help me find the decorations in the basement."

Through the living-room window I see Smokey pawing impatiently at the ground. "We have to take Smokey back to the barn."

Cid and Queenie look disappointed, so I tell them just to stay with Ma and help decorate the tree. I pretend that I'm put out, but I really don't mind taking Smokey back by myself. In fact, I'm looking forward to having some time alone.

"Watch out for Clem," Cid moans in a ghostly voice from the top of the basement stairs.

"Ha, ha. Funny." I tighten my scarf and slip outside. I can hear Ma asking Cid who Clem is, and Queenie shouting that she found the box of ornaments, before I close the door and leave the warmth and the bustle of the house behind.

a chance meeting

The sun is already low in the sky, throwing long gray shadows across the yard. A snowplow thunders down the street, pushing the snow to one side and spraying salt everywhere. Smokey shakes his head. The little pinecones dance around on the ends of the ribbons. I unhitch the sled and remove the harness. I lean the sled against the side of the house, then remove the Gorilla's noseband and stuff it in my coat pocket.

Through the living-room window I see Ma and Queenie and Cid pulling out decorations from our old Christmas box and placing them carefully on the tree. The fire is leaping in the fireplace, the orange flames illuminating the tree and everyone's faces. If you didn't know any better, you would say that we were the happiest family in the world. You wouldn't know about frozen pipes and electric bills and everything. You'd think we were near perfect, decorating the tree, waiting for our father to come home from work and tell us about his day.

I watch through the window, until Smokey nudges me in the side with his muzzle. I run my hand down his neck, then lead him to the sidewalk and into the street. The plow has left a clean swath on one side of the road. I lead Smokey close to the curb just in case a car should come along. It's near dinnertime, and all the houses are lit up and cheerful. As we walk along, Smokey's gentle movement lulls me deeper in thought. His breath is warm, the steam curling around my hand. We're going along like this when I hear a familiar voice call my name.

"Hey, Nathaniel!"

I turn to see Cheryl Hanson coming toward me, a big smile on her face. She walks right up to me, her eyelashes lightly frosted beneath her green cap, her heart-shaped face rosy and beautiful from the cold. My heart stops beating in my chest and my mouth goes instantly dry.

"Is this your horse? She's beautiful."

"He's a he, actually," I say, trying to keep my voice from cracking.

"What's his name?"

"Smokey."

"Did you do this?" She points at the ribbons and tinsel.

I can feel myself start to blush. "My little sister. She treats him like a Barbie doll sometimes."

"I think it's really pretty. May I pet him?"

She looks at me so sweetly. I tell myself to stay calm. "Sure. He's gentle. Like a big dog. Here . . ." I hand her a piece of apple from my coat pocket. "You can feed him if you like. You'll be his friend for life."

Cheryl takes the apple and holds it up. Smokey tries to grab it with his mouth, and Cheryl pulls her hand away in fright.

"No, like this." I show her how to hold her hand flat so that Smokey won't nip her accidentally.

She holds the apple out again, only this time with a flat hand like I showed her. Smokey nuzzles the apple, then takes it, crunching it noisily.

"He really likes it!" Cheryl says, laughing.

"Yeah. Like I said, he's just like a big dog." I ruffle Smokey's mane and scratch his forehead roughly with my mittened hand.

"Where are you taking him?"

"Back to the barn. We had him pull our Christmas tree to the house." I can't help saying this with some pride in my voice. How many other kids have a pony to deliver a Christmas tree to their house?

"Do you want some company?"

"Where?" I stupidly ask.

"Taking him back to the barn. I don't have anything else to do."

"Won't your folks wonder where you are?"

"They've gone visiting relatives. Cousins three times removed that I don't even know or care about." She squinches up her face.

I laugh a little too loudly at this, then check myself right away, but at this point I'm nearly screaming inside my skull. I want to jump around and whip snowballs at stop signs or something, but force myself to play it cool instead. This would be easier if my voice didn't suddenly crack all over the place and make me sound like a goof. "It's . . . it's really far. We won't be back before dark."

Cheryl is sweet and pretends she doesn't notice my voice breaking or my face turning all red.

"That's OK. I'm free for at least a couple of hours."

And so I find myself walking with the most beautiful girl in school on the most beautiful night in December, and I can't believe my luck. The snow is falling gently all around us. We walk along, talking about school and music and movies, and I'm amazed to find out we like so many of the same things—even though we live on different planets. Suddenly, I get an idea.

"Do you want to ride him?"

"What?"

"He won't mind. We ride him all the time. It's fun. He'll keep you warm, too."

Cheryl blinks as she considers this. "But he hasn't got a saddle on or anything."

"It's all right. He's really comfortable—like a big soft chair. Here, I'll give you a leg up." I help her grab a handful of Smokey's mane, then hold out my hands for her knee. I notice my finger sticking out of a hole in my mitten, so I whip my mittens off quickly and stuff them into my coat pocket. I hold my bare hands out for her instead, and she just looks at me.

"It's OK," I reassure her. "I do this for my sisters all the time. Come on."

She places her knee delicately in my hands, and I lift her up onto Smokey's back. "Just keep hold of his mane like that and you'll be fine."

Cheryl balances nervously on top of Smokey, holding his mane tight in her gloved hands.

"How does that feel?" I ask her.

"Good . . . It feels good . . . I think!" She laughs nervously, her eyes shining brightly in the evening light.

"Just let your legs relax, but try not to swing them around and kick him." I cluck with my tongue to get Smokey up. I can't think of a thing to say once Cheryl stops talking, so I lead Smokey along in silence. I look back occasionally to see Cheryl smiling happily at me. We walk like this for some time, until we come to the top of the hill where the lane to the barn begins. The snow has drifted in big unbroken arcs across the lane.

"Maybe I should get off him now," Cheryl says.

"No, stay on. The snow is really deep. They don't plow it."

Smokey picks his way along the lane, lifting his feet high to clear the drifts. Some are so deep, they touch his belly. I tell Cheryl to hang on extra-tight, because Smokey has to rabbit-jump to make it through. She looks a bit scared as Smokey clears the first drift, me leaping by his side. When we reach the barn, I hold my hand out to help Cheryl down. She leans over and puts her arm around my neck instead, her warm face nearly touching mine.

"That was so much fun!" she says.

"Here, can you hold him for a minute?" I hand Cheryl the lead and she takes it willingly. I open the barn door, then feel around for the switch. For the first time since we've been boarding Smokey here, I don't think about Clem's ghost before I turn on the light. The horses look up from their feed bins, munching serenely on their hay. I take Smokey's lead from Cheryl, who hesitates at the door.

"Come on in. It's OK."

"It's kind of spooky. Do you always come here alone?"

"Sometimes. There's supposed to be a ghost in here." I say this just to impress her.

"Really?"

"Yeah. Some old guy named Clem who used to live in the barn with his pigs. He fell off a beam and broke his neck." I don't tell her about how he used to chase us with a bullwhip for playing in the hay when we were kids.

"Doesn't that scare you? I'd be terrified to come here by myself." She wraps her arms around her chest and shivers. "I don't like ghosts and things like that. It creeps me out to think about them."

"It doesn't bother me," I boast.

The story of Clem's ghost must have Cheryl pretty scared, because she's practically walking in my boots as I lead Smokey into his stall. She follows behind and stands with one hand on Smokey's back—the same way Queenie does—while I remove his halter. The *Star Wars* theme is playing on the radio. For some reason, Cheryl finds this funny.

"The horses like the sound of the radio," I explain. "It keeps them calm."

"Do they pick the station?" She gives me a wry smile.

"No. They'd listen to disco if I let them."

We laugh together at this, our eyes meeting for a moment. Cheryl looks away, then runs her hand along Smokey's neck.

"Should we take the ribbons from his hair?"

I look at Smokey, the pinecones dangling from his mane and tail. "I guess so. He'd just get them tangled and ruin all my sister's hard work."

We stand close to each other, our hands almost touching as we work the tinsel and ribbons from

Smokey's mane. Cheryl has taken her gloves off, and her fingers move quickly. She removes the ribbons easily, holding them in a bunch in one of her hands. I don't know why, but I can't stop smiling. Cheryl must think I'm crazy.

"You're good at this," I finally say.

"I braid my sister's hair all the time. I love this sort of thing." She moves to Smokey's tail and begins removing the ribbons there, too. She doesn't even hesitate to stand behind him, as though she'd been working around horses all her life. She hands me the ribbons when she's through. I shove them in my coat pockets as well.

"I have to brush him," I tell her. "Do you want to help?"

She nods and I hand her the currycomb. I show her how to use it and how to clean it by banging it out against the floor. I pick Smokey's feet, while Cheryl works away at brushing him, a serious look on her face. When she's done, I throw the old blanket over Smokey, securing it at his chest and under his belly with clothespins. I stand up to find Cheryl looking right at me.

"You shouldn't be afraid to speak up in class, Nathaniel. You're really smart and it's OK if the other kids look dumb. They wish they were smart like you. You shouldn't hide it."

I'm listening to what she's saying, but all I can think is that I've never heard my name sound so good before.

"You're so lucky to have a horse," she continues, as though it's totally normal for her and me to be together like this. "I've been bugging my parents for a horse since I was a little kid, but they'll never let me get one."

"How come?" I say, finally finding my voice. "It's not like they can't afford it."

"They can afford it, all right. They just won't. My dad thinks it's too dangerous. Like I'm going to fall and break my neck or something. I bet your dad doesn't hassle you like that. . . ."

She realizes too late what she's said. "Oh, I'm sorry . . . I forgot. . . ."

I shrug to let her know I don't care, even though I can feel my face starting to flush again. I know she didn't say it to be mean. I know the whole school knows our business. Actually, I'm more surprised to hear her speak so strongly about her parents. I always thought rich kids had perfect families and got everything they wanted. Hearing that Cheryl wants a horse

151

and can't have one has a strange effect on me. I find myself saying something that Cid and Queenie would kill me for.

"You can come here anytime and ride Smokey."

Cheryl looks at me with her big, innocent eyes. "That's really sweet of you to offer."

"I'm serious. You can come with me anytime you want. I mean . . . as long as your boyfriend doesn't mind."

"My boyfriend?"

"Tyler. The guy who gives you rides home from school all the time. He's your boyfriend, isn't he?"

Her face shows shock and then disgust. "Tyler? He's not my boyfriend. He just wishes he was. I don't have a boyfriend right now."

She says this last part with her nose in the air, as though she's proud of it. I can't believe my ears. I feel like Christmas has come early. I don't know if she's telling me the truth or not, and I don't care. Suddenly I want to tell her everything. I want to tell her that I love her and that she's the most beautiful girl I've ever seen. I want to tell her that I dream about her and think about her all the time and that I've never felt this way about anyone before.

Of course, I don't say any of this. What I do say is

that there are other horses in the barn she may like to see. So we walk down the aisles, one stall after the other, me telling her all the names of the different horses and what I know about their personalities and owners. I show her the palominos and the Gorilla's colt. I tell her all about how the big ape forced us to get Smokey gelded. I even mimic his voice for her, which makes her laugh. But when I go to return the noseband to its rightful place, I discover a padlock on the Gorilla's tack box. I don't know what to do, so I stuff the noseband back in my pocket. Then I show Cheryl Silver and Flag, the horse Smokey defeated on his first day in the field. And finally, at the very end, I show her Jed. He weaves back and forth when we walk by. I tell Cheryl how his owner never feeds him or waters him, let alone brushes him.

"Why does he keep him?" she asks in horror.

"I don't know. He doesn't understand him or even like him. He just likes owning him so he can brag to all his friends."

"It's so cruel! I can't stand it!"

The tears well in Cheryl's eyes.

"We feed and water him," I reassure her. "I'd clean out his stall and brush him, too, but he's wild. He won't let me near him."

This seems to make her feel better. She wipes her tears away and you can barely tell she's been crying. Then she slips her small, warm hand in mine.

"You're really nice, Nat."

I can feel my heart beating in my throat and in my ears. My face is hot and my hands are all sweaty. I hope she can't tell these changes are happening to me. I hope I just seem normal and that I don't look like I'm going to explode, which is how I feel. She moves closer to me. I can't even hear what I'm saying, but the next thing I know her mouth is against mine. Her lips are firm and warm and taste like strawberries. I kiss her back and she laughs, which makes me wonder if I'm doing it right or not. I've never kissed a girl before—other than Ma and my sisters, but that doesn't count. This is entirely different—like electricity arcing, or lightning shooting between us. This kissing feels dangerous and I want it to go on all night. . . .

And then we're walking hand in hand through the snow to the road. Somehow I managed to turn out the lights in the barn and close the door, but I can't really remember doing any of it. Cheryl starts to run, pulling me along by the hand through the drifts. We run like this, laughing wildly, and then we stumble and fall into the snow. She leans over and kisses me again, only this time softly and more slowly.

"Close your eyes," she says.

I close my eyes and feel her lips against my mouth. Then she pushes a handful of cold snow in my face.

"Hey! You little brat!"

Cheryl jumps up and runs. I chase her, letting her stay just an arm's length away, even though I could catch her in a second. She screams and throws snowballs at me, which I easily dodge, and then I tackle her and knock her into a big drift. I hold a handful of snow over her head.

"Say uncle!"

"No!"

"Say uncle!" I hold the snow higher like I'm going to slam it in her face.

"You wouldn't dare, Nathaniel!"

She looks at me so innocently with those blue eyes of hers that my heart melts all inside my chest. I drop the snow and lean over to kiss her some more, but she pushes me away and jumps to her feet. I jump up after her and grab her hand, and we walk in the falling snow, all the way through town and to her street. It's strange, but everything seems different and new to me. The streetlamps glow peacefully. The windows of the houses cast a warm amber light. I want to turn and look at Cheryl a million times while we're walking, but I stop myself in case I break whatever spell the night is under. I just love her smile and, what's more, I can't believe she's smiling at me.

When we reach the corner of her street, she pulls me to an abrupt stop.

"I'd better say good-bye here. My folks are kind of crazy about who I hang around with."

She sees my expression and starts to apologize.

"It's not that . . . It's just . . . they don't know you."

"Sure. I understand."

I understand all too well. They don't want their princess daughter being seen with the likes of me. But I can't hold her responsible for the way her parents feel. It's not fair to her. I lean toward her to give her a kiss, but she puts her hand on my chest and pats my coat.

"Thanks again for the nice time. I had fun."

And then she turns and walks down the street. She walks through the falling snow, past the expensive homes and the four-car garages. She walks in and out of the streetlights like an angel appearing and disappearing before me. I watch her grow smaller and smaller, until she slips into a shadow and is gone.

I stand there for a long time, wishing the night weren't over. I want to turn back the clock and stay with Cheryl and Smokey in the barn forever. I go on thinking like this, my eyes closed, imagining the touch and the taste of her lips against my mouth. I do this until my feet get so cold I can't feel my toes anymore. And then I turn and run home. I don't mind the cold biting at my lungs and face. I run so fast, I can't even feel my feet touch the ground. When I get in front of the house, I can see our Christmas tree twinkling through the living-room window.

"You were gone a long while," Ma says when I puff into the house. "I thought we were going to have to go out looking for you."

"I just took my time, is all."

I can feel Ma looking at me kind of funny. I bet she knows something is up. I take my boots off and hang up my coat slower than usual so I have time to settle down.

"Come and look at Douglas!" Queenie shouts from the living room. "He's the best tree ever."

Cid, Queenie, and Ma are gathered around the fire

admiring the tree. It looks beautiful, despite our mish-mash of old ornaments. Somehow Ma always manages to make everything look good.

"It's beautiful," I say, and I mean it, although it could have looked like anything and I would have said the same thing. I can't stop thinking about Cheryl and the night. The whole thing seems like a dream.

"How's Smokey?" Cid asks.

"He's great. He's really good." I guess I answer too enthusiastically because she turns and looks at me kind of funny, too. Our eyes meet, and I can't stop the happiness from showing on my face. Cid and I just look at each other long and hard, and then she raises her eyebrows and turns away.

"I saved you some hot chocolate," she says, getting up and going toward the kitchen.

I follow her and stand next to the stove as she ladles the hot chocolate into a mug. "I won't ask," she says, handing me the mug. "Be careful. It's hot."

"I'll tell you sometime. I promise."

"It's OK. I'm sure I'll find out sooner or later."

Normally I would take this as a threat, but I can tell by Cid's voice that she is letting me off the hook. I'm tempted to tell her all about Cheryl—about how nice she is and everything—but part of me wants to keep the night to myself, to hold on to the magic as long as I can and not spoil it with words.

"Thanks, Cid. I mean it."

We walk back into the living room and join Queenie and Ma on the couch by the fire. I drink my hot chocolate quickly, then sneak up to my bed because I'm restless and I want to be alone. Tomorrow is Friday, the last day of school before Christmas, and the sooner I get to sleep, the sooner I see Cheryl in the morning. But I end up lying in bed staring at the ceiling, replaying the evening with Cheryl over and over. I know this sounds stupid, but I imagine all kinds of things—like me and Cheryl going steady and even getting married and having kids. I imagine everything, like what kind of dog we'll have and even what kind of car we'll drive. I'm still thinking about this by the time Queenie and Cid rustle up the stairs to bed.

the spell breaks

I get up earlier than usual the next day because I want to look as good as I can for school. Earlier than usual means half an hour before school, which means I'll be late for the bell all the same. My heart is still skipping beats from the night before. But when I go to use the bathroom, Cid has already beaten me to it and I know I'm sunk. It takes her hours to get ready just to go to the corner store. Now I can't even grab my comb or brush my teeth. I bang on the door with my fist.

"Hurry up, disco queen! You've been in there for hours." Cid hates disco. She's a David Bowie fan.

"I just got in here. You can wait."

"I have to get ready for school!"

"So do I! I'll be out when I'm ready."

I pace back and forth in front of the door, hating Cid's guts again. How can she do this to me? "Hurry up! I have to get in there!"

Silence. Cid doesn't even grace me with an answer this time.

"Fine! I'll remember this, Cid!" I kick the door, cursing the day she was born. I crash back to my room and dig through a pile of dirty clothes on the floor at the foot of my bed, trying to find my good velour shirt—the one Ma embroidered with my initials. I can hear Ma's words running through my head about how I should keep my room clean and how I'm old enough to do my own laundry. Now I understand why she says these things to me. I dig and dig but I can't find my shirt. "Aaaaahhhhhhh!"

I kick my pile of old Spider-Man comics across the room in frustration. I can hear the time ticking away on my bedside alarm clock. I find my best pair of jeans, shake them out, and jump into them. I sift through the clothes and find a pair of matching socks. I check my hair in the mirror and realize I'm screwed. My hair looks like a chicken tail, sticking every which way. And to make matters worse, I have a big pimple forming on my upper lip. I hate those ones. They hurt so much. *At least it isn't on my nose,* I think, *knock on wood.*

Just then, the door to the bathroom smashes open. Cid tries to sneak past me and tear down the stairs—because she's wearing my velour shirt!

"Hey! Take it off!"

Cid grabs her coat and flies out the door. She has her boots on already, so she leaves me standing there, screaming like an idiot through the front door.

"You stupid jerk! I'm going to wreck all your stuff!"

Ma would kill me if she heard me yelling out the door like some hooligan, but she's already at work, so she won't know. It'd be no use trying to explain to Ma that Cid took my best shirt, anyway. She'd just tell me to go put on something else and get on with it. There isn't much justice in our house. Not the right kind, at least. But I'll get Cid back. . . .

I run up the stairs and jump into the bathroom. Queenie is in there sitting on the toilet, still in her pajamas. She doesn't mind if I come in and brush my teeth.

"What's all the yelling about?" she asks, rubbing the sleep from her eyes.

"Oh, nothing. Just Cid. I'm going to break her neck. Hurry up, Queenie, or we're going to be late." I splash water on my hair and try to get it to sit down. Then I revisit my pile of dirty clothes and look for the next best thing to wear. Everything is either full of holes or wrinkled beyond recognition. I pick a dress shirt with sleeves that are too short and roll them up to my elbows. I throw a shrunken green wool vest on top of this and check myself in the mirror. Terrible. But it will have to do.

When I'm finished primping, Queenie is still moping about in her pink fuzzies. "Come on, Queenie, let's go."

"I don't have anything to wear."

"Just throw on anything. Wear what you wore yesterday."

"I wore what I wore yesterday for three days already."

"Well, wear it again!"

I leave her to get ready while I smooth more water on my hair and check my teeth. At last Queenie's ready. We bundle up and fly out the door. I all but drag her down the street to school. Queenie starts to dip and skip like she's going to dance, and I yank her arm a bit.

"You're hurting my hand, Nat!"

"There's no time for dancing!"

Queenie looks betrayed. I feel like a big jerk, but I can't help it. I hear the bell from across the park.

"Jeez. Come on, Queenie!"

I make Queenie trot to her schoolyard and push her through the gate. Then I run across the street to my own school. The national anthem is already playing as I skid up to my homeroom door. The teacher gives me a dirty look, so I stand to one side of the door, out of her field of vision. When the anthem stops, I slip into the class and try to take my seat unnoticed. The teacher doesn't even say my name; she just points at me.

"Office."

"But—"

"Go."

I groan, then get up to go.

"Take your books with you. Homeroom will be over before you get back."

Right. I grab my books and hurry down the hall. The last person I want to see is old Turtle Neck, our principal. We call him that because his head melts right into his neck, and it's all wrinkled, like a turtle's. On top of that, he's slow. He couldn't move fast if someone lit his pants on fire, which I've thought of doing more than once.

Anyway, I want to get to history class early to talk to Cheryl alone before all the other kids show up. But Turtle Neck keeps me waiting, asking all kinds of stupid questions that nobody needs answers to, like how many times was I late this semester, and doesn't my mother work over at such-and-such law firm. I can feel myself growing old in Turtle Neck's office. I feel like I'm going to start smashing things as I watch the minute hand on the clock practically spin around its face.

At last he lets me go, and I run to class. I'm sure my hair is a mess again, and I can feel the sweat under my arms. Mrs. Malanus shoots me a look as I flip the late slip on her desk and take my seat without looking at the rest of the class. The kids snicker. I check the fly of my jeans just to be sure. It's closed.

I take the time to collect myself and organize my books. I look over the shoulder of the kid in front of me to see what page we're on, then settle in. When enough time has passed for the class to forget about my late entry, I turn slightly in my chair to look over at Cheryl. I have to do it casually so she doesn't think I'm a weirdo. I decide to use the old pencil-drop distraction to accomplish my mission. The pencil hits the floor as planned, but bounces funny on its eraser and flips up to the front of the class, rolling to a stop in front of Mrs. Malanus's desk. She sneers over the top of her bifocals like she just ate a piece of bad cheese.

"When you're ready, Mr. Estabrooks . . ."

The class snickers again, and I can feel my face turn red. I retrieve my pencil and slink back to my seat. I sit staring straight ahead until I can't stand it anymore and finally decide to just turn around and look at Cheryl in her seat at the back of the class. Will she be wearing her tight blue sweater? Will her hair be up in a ponytail or down around her face? I run my hand through my hair, then slowly turn in my seat. But she's not there! My heart sinks as I sit there staring at her empty desk.

"Did you lose something, Mr. Estabrooks?"

"No, ma'am."

I turn forward in my seat, my hopes dashed. Where could she be? Why didn't she come to school today?

The rest of the morning drags on and on until I think I'm going to go crazy. I don't even want to watch the special film the teachers rented for us as a

Christmas treat. I bide my time just long enough, then slip through the school doors and run to the park. I feel so disappointed about Cheryl that I don't even care if I get in trouble. I don't care if Turtle Neck himself comes looking for me. I kick my way along the path toward home, scheming ways to meet up with Cheryl over Christmas vacation. I think about delivering something to her house, or walking past her place over and over, or even bringing Smokey downtown and right to her doorstep to take her for a ride. I laugh at this idea, then think it may not be a bad one at all.

That's when I notice two figures bundled close together, sitting on the old cannons at the gate to the park. Two kids playing hooky, I tell myself. Guess they didn't want to watch some stupid Christmas film either. But when I get closer to the cannons, I can see that it's Cheryl and Tyler. There's no mistaking that they're together. Cheryl doesn't even see me, because she's got her mouth planted right on Tyler's lips.

In an instant, the thin web connecting our worlds is broken and I can feel the rage filling up inside me. I want to knock them both off the cannons. I want to call Cheryl every bad name I can think of. I want to beat Tyler to a pulp so that he can never kiss another girl again.

But all I do is walk past them, staring like a helpless fool. I know Cheryl sees me, because our eyes meet for a second. She pretends not to notice me and goes on kissing Tyler. I keep on walking until I'm at least two blocks beyond the park. And then I run. I run as hard and as fast as I've ever run in my life. I want to keep running until I can't breathe anymore, until I'm blind and deaf and never want to love anyone ever again. I can feel my heart bursting inside my chest, and I'm sure I'm going to die. That will show her! I imagine myself dead and stretched out in the street, the police cars blocking the road, and Cheryl crying hysterically at my feet because it's her fault that I'm gone.

When I get home, I barely kick my boots off before stumbling up the stairs to my room. I slam my door, throw myself on my bed, and bury my face in my pillow. I try to be strong and not care, but it doesn't work. I can feel the tears running down my face. "That witch. That little witch!"

It's all I can do to keep from sobbing like a girl. But it's my fault, really. Why would someone like

Cheryl Hanson have anything to do with a guy like me? I must have been out of my skull to think that she would like me, let alone want to be my girlfriend. But why did she kiss me, then? My heart feels like it's ripped in half. I glare at the yellowed ceiling in my room. It's nothing like the color of daffodils, I think. It's the color of neglect. The fist hits me in the stomach again and the whole room seems to breathe in and out around me. I lie like this for hours, until Ma comes and taps on my door.

"Nathaniel, are you all right? Your people are calling wondering where their papers are."

That's what Ma calls my paper-route customers— my people. Of course they want to know where their stupid papers are, I think. Heaven forbid they should miss a day of breaking news in this stupid town. If "my people" had real lives, they wouldn't be so concerned about their damn papers. "I'm sick," I call out.

Ma opens the door and peers in. "What's the matter?"

I turn my face to the wall so she won't see that I've been crying. "I don't know. A cold or something, I think." I sniff a couple of times as proof.

"You sound all stuffed up." Ma comes across the room and puts her cool hand on my head. "You feel kind of hot. I'd better take your temperature."

"I'm fine, Ma. I just need some rest."

"How about a bath and a cup of tea? That'll make you feel better."

"Sure. Fine. Whatever. I'll be all right."

"I'll tell Cid and Queenie to deliver your papers tonight. They know the route, right?"

"Yeah. They've delivered them for me before."

Ma leaves the room. I can hear her drawing the bath. She comes back and sticks her head through the door. "Go on and jump in. I'll bring you some tea when it's ready."

I really don't want a bath or tea, but I can't tell Ma that. She'll just poke and pry until she finds out why I'm really in bed. I lower myself into the steaming tub, the water so hot it's barely tolerable. That's Ma's way. She believes in the power of a good boil to heal whatever ails. I must admit, feeling the hot water against my skin does make me feel a little bit better. I splash my face, delicately at first, then more vigorously as I get used to the temperature. Finally, I sink right down in the tub until just my eyes and nose are sticking above the water like an old alligator's.

Through the water I hear a bang on the door. I sit up with a loud *splash*. It must be Ma with my tea. There's another bang on the door, but this time louder and angrier.

"I need to get in there!"

It's Cid, wanting to perform some mysterious and lengthy bathroom ritual. I take the opportunity for a little revenge. I sink back into the water.

"I just got in. I don't know how long I'll be."

"I need to get my things from in there."

"Well, that's tough! I'll come out when I'm ready!"

No sooner do I say these words than the door is kicked open, sending the rickety dead bolt flying across the bathroom. The door swings helplessly on its hinges as Cid marches across the floor like a queen. I can't believe she would do this, and I just sit there in shock, gripping the shower curtain around me, my mouth gaping open. She gathers her things imperiously, then marches back out. She doesn't even have the decency to shut the door.

Then Ma appears with my tea. "What happened to the lock?" she asks.

I wrench the shower curtain shut in disgust. "Can't anyone have any privacy around here?!"

Ma leaves the tea on the edge of the tub, and

closes the door on her way out. I sit in the tub fuming over how I'm going to get Cid back. I think about smashing all her little glass animal figurines that Dad gave her over the years. I think about cutting holes in all her socks or putting glue in her hair or something. I'm so mad thinking about how I'm going to wreck Cid's life that I forget to think about Cheryl and Tyler. At least for now.

broken glass

By the time I decide what I'm going to do to Cid, my anger has cooled, for the most part. I can't hold a grudge the way Cid can, and I can't run crying to Ma the way Queenie does when her feelings are hurt. So I've learned to think my anger out and let it go. Looking at Cid's little figurines all neatly arranged on her dresser, I can't bring myself to actually smash them. So I wrap them in toilet paper and hide them behind her dresser. And then I wait.

I sit on my bed reading. It's long past dark before I hear Cid and Queenie bustle in from delivering my papers. I hear them call out to let Ma know they're home, then hear them tramp up the stairs. I wait like a spider for my victim. Cid and Queenie go into their room, and it's Queenie who first notices the figurines are missing. Cid figures out immediately that I'm at the bottom of this diabolical abduction.

"Nathaniel, you scumbag! What did you do with them?"

I look up from my book like I have no idea what she's talking about.

"Don't play dumb! Where are my animals?"

"Your animals? I have no idea what you're talking about."

"Yes, you do, you liar! Give them back!"

"I don't have them."

Cid storms out of my room, and I can hear her opening and closing her dresser drawers in a frenzy, searching for the figurines. Suddenly she screams and starts kicking her dresser in frustration. I jump out of bed to try to stop her.

"Cut it out, you psycho!"

"Where are they? Where did you put them?"

She grabs me by the shirt, but I knock her hand away. "I'm not going to tell you until you back off! And I want you to say sorry for kicking the door in today."

She lets go of my shirt and folds her arms across

her chest. She stares at me, her eyes burning with hatred. "Fine! I'm sorry. Now, where are they?"

I feel like making her grovel, but for some reason I think better of it. "Just keep your hands off me," I warn her as I reach behind the dresser. I feel around for the toilet paper bundle and pull it out. "Here are your precious little animals."

I hand the bundle to Cid, who quickly unwraps the figurines. But when she opens the bundle, the little animals are smashed into a million pieces. Cid's jaw drops and then her face collapses. "My animals!"

"Oh, no!" Queenie gasps.

Cid looks up at me in disbelief. "How could you? How could you do it? My poor little animals."

She sits down on her bed and starts to cry like I haven't seen her do since she was little. I feel sick to my stomach again. I'm glad I didn't make her grovel, at least.

"I didn't mean for them to smash, Cid. Honest. I only meant to make you mad for a bit. I didn't know you would go crazy and kick the dresser. We can fix them. Here. Give them to me."

Cid just sits there sobbing, holding the animals delicately in their toilet paper shroud. I take the bundle from her and inspect the damage. The figurines are shattered beyond repair, with only a few horse and sheep heads still intact.

"I'm so sorry, Cid. I'll make it up to you. I promise."

Cid doesn't answer. She falls back on her bed and cries into her pillow. I look over to Queenie for understanding, but she just stares at me, and I can tell by her eyes what she is thinking of me. I feel like the biggest creep on the planet, and there's nothing I can do but leave the room in shame. I feel doubly bad because Cid had delivered my papers, like Ma asked.

Suddenly it doesn't matter that she stole my best shirt and kicked in the bathroom door. It doesn't matter that she's a big boss all of the time and drives me crazy. None of these things matter, because what I've done can't be fixed. All I can do is lie in bed and hate myself for the rest of the night.

I wake up the next morning with an idea in my head. It's Saturday—only two days before Christmas. But I still have time to right the wrong I did to Cid. I decide to skip breakfast altogether so I can hit the road early. I leave a note on the kitchen table telling Cid and Queenie to go to the barn alone. Then I bundle up, grab my carrier bag, and walk across town to the newspaper depot.

The back doors are open at the depot, and I can see the papers flying in a giant newsprint ribbon on the machine. The men working inside quickly bind the papers into bundles as they come off the press, thumping them into tall piles at the front of the warehouse. The air smells heavily of grease and ink. The machines are so loud that the men communicate through gestures and nods. One of them notices me standing by the door. He whistles to another man and points at me. The man walks over to where I'm standing. He's carrying a clipboard. His hands are stained black with ink.

"Can I help you?" he shouts over the machines.

"I want to pick my papers up early. I don't want to wait for the truck to drop them off." I lift my carrier bag to show him that I'm legitimate.

The man gestures toward the stacks of papers. "I got a million papers here, kid. I don't know which bundle is yours."

"I need seventy-two. Just tell the driver I picked them up."

"Which driver?"

"Bill. The old guy. He drives a brown van."

"You think I know everybody?" He turns as though to walk away.

"Look, it's just this once. I've got to get these papers out before the stores close. Please, mister." I look at him with my neediest face. I'm not sure if he will budge, because he doesn't look like the kind of guy who budges very often.

"My mom's sick. I have to get to the store," I say.

The man stares at me sceptically, then dismisses me with a wave of his clipboard. He rubs his head with his inky hand, then shakes his head. "Wait here."

He walks over to the piles of newspapers, grabs a couple of bundles, and hauls them back to where I'm standing. He drops them heavily at my feet.

"Thanks, mister. My mom will be grateful."

"Yeah, whatever. Merry Christmas, kid."

I use my house key to cut the plastic tape that holds the papers together. They feel warm and smell of fresh ink. I shove the papers into my bag, then hurry across the road and back toward my neighborhood. My "people" are curious and happy that I'm delivering their papers so early—except for Mrs. Geeter, who's grouchier than ever. She eyes me suspiciously and counts her money several times before giving it to me. But aside from her, pretty much everyone gives me a tip. I'm my most cheerful self, wishing everyone a merry Christmas as I pocket the money. I count fifteen dollars in tips alone. That's almost five dollars more than last year. I practically run through my route, finishing in record time. I have to hurry to catch the bus to the mall. Tomorrow is Christmas Eve and all the stores will close early.

I race over to the bus station and catch the bus just as it's pulling out of the station. I hand the driver a two-dollar bill, and he hands it back to me.

"Exact change only."

I pull out a handful of change from my collection money, then carefully count out the right amount. I throw it in the change box, the coins rattling noisily down its metal throat. The driver shuts the door behind me and steps on the gas, sending me flying before I have a chance to find a seat.

The bus is packed with holiday shoppers and their runny-nosed kids. There are people standing in the aisle, holding the metal rail that runs along the ceiling of the bus. Their faces are somber, not at all what you would expect for the season. They swing back and forth with the movements of the bus, like meat hanging in a freezer truck. There is one seat free—a window seat next to a big, grumpy-looking woman with bags and boxes at her feet. She sighs as I apologize, stepping over her and into the spot. I could have stood in the aisle, too, but I don't want to look like meat in a freezer truck. I want to look out the window at the decorations and things.

All the houses and shops in town are decorated with lights and ribbons and ornaments. One house even has its door wrapped up to look like a Christmas present. In many of the house windows you can see Christmas trees standing proudly. I feel happy, despite everything that's happened over the past few days. Then I think about the harness I was going to buy for Smokey with my collection money. That will have to wait now.

The bus leaves our small town behind and careens along country roads for about fifteen minutes. The air is stuffy and hot. The grumpy woman seems to be getting bigger by the minute. Her legs and shoulders are pressing me into the side of the bus. I can hear her breathing heavily beside me. She digs a candy out of her purse, her elbow stabbing me in the ribs. She rustles the wrapper loud and long before finally stuffing the candy in her mouth. I turn my back to her, just slightly, to let her know I'm uncomfortable. She takes the opportunity to take up even more space. I feel like I'm going to die by the time the bus finally pulls up to the mall and opens its doors.

Of course, the grumpy woman waits until everyone is off the bus before she struggles out with her bags and boxes. When I step outside at last, I breathe deeply, taking in the cold, fresh air. I see the woman still struggling with her things, trying to juggle all the packages. I watch her for a bit, then offer to get her a shopping cart, even though I just want to get on with my own shopping. But it's Christmas, I tell myself. She thanks me profusely, then presses a quarter into my hand like it's a gold doubloon. I think of something smart to say, but just wish her a merry Christmas instead and light out for the stores before she asks me to push the cart for her or something.

The mall is packed with people. Holiday music blares over the sound system as bodies struggle to move from store to store. I am swept up in the stream, merging with the rest of the shoppers. When I reach the jewelry store, I break out of the flow. The store is lit up like a doctor's office with shining glass displays and women who look like mannequins behind the counters. There are mostly men in the store, buying rings and things for their girlfriends and wives. A young woman with too much makeup and straight black hair to her waist smiles at me.

"Can I help you find something?"

"I'm looking for glass figurines."

She motions me to the back wall of the store and points to a display of Royal Doulton figures. There are shelves and shelves of pretty young women in expensive Victorian dresses doing everything from gazing at birds to swinging on swings. I shake my head.

"I'm looking for figurines of animals. Horses and sheep and things."

The woman thinks for a minute, then reaches below one of the counters.

"We have these."

She holds up a tiny white glass greyhound with three tiny white greyhound puppies strapped together with a fine gold chain.

"Is that all you have?"

The woman nods.

"How much is it?"

She checks the small tag on the bottom of the figurine. "Twenty-five dollars."

"What?!"

Ma would deck me if she heard me respond like this, but I can't help it. Twenty-five dollars is more than I've got. And it's not even what I wanted to buy for Cid. I was hoping to come home with several horses and things that she liked, not a bunch of prissy greyhounds tied together with a fancy chain.

"Would you like to think about it?" the woman asks me.

"Yes. I'm going to look around a bit. I really had my heart set on a horse."

I move from store to store, maneuvering through the holiday shoppers. I've become as desperate as the rest of them. The stores are practically empty, the best things already sold and gone. The horses and sheep that I do manage to find are too big and too expensive.

After an hour and a half of searching, I'm ready to give up. I've checked every store in the mall. At the last minute, I drop into a card shop—just in case. The store isn't as busy as the rest. A white-haired woman arranges candles in one of the aisles. I scan the store quickly and decide there's nothing for me.

Great. I'm done. I'll never find anything for Cid. Then I catch a glimpse of a tiny wicker basket on one of the glass shelves. I look inside the basket and discover a small porcelain fawn curled up with a tiny blanket as though sleeping. The basket with the fawn is so small, it fits neatly in the palm of my hand. I don't even ask about the price but bring it right up to the counter, where the white-haired lady rings it in.

"Eight fifty-nine."

I count out the money eagerly and hand it to the woman. "Do you have a small box?"

"I have some tissue paper. Will that do?"

I walk out of the store with the fawn wrapped in tissue paper in a small brown bag. I'm so happy I found it, and happier still that I have enough money left over to buy the presents I want to get for Queenie and Ma. I've been planning all along to buy both the black and silver hoof polish for Queenie. And Ma will get bath salts like every year, but I have enough money to buy her some nice soap and maybe a candle to go with it.

I see the bus pulling up to the stop, so I run to catch it. I jostle with the other people, this time taking an aisle seat. It's dark now and there's nothing to see anyway. I'm so excited about the fawn that the bus ride goes by quickly. When we get back to town, the snow is falling again in big white flakes that dance in the light from the streetlamps. I walk home slowly, enjoying the night, my newspaper bag still slung over my shoulder and resting against my thigh.

Walking in the snow like this reminds me of the time that Dad saved Christmas. He used to do all kinds of things to amaze us, like light his hands on fire without getting burned, or peel the layers from a golf ball so we could play with the rubber ball inside. But the most amazing thing he ever did was make it snow one Christmas Eve. We were really little. We told Dad we wanted snow. He called the weatherman to tell him he had three kids who wanted a white Christmas, and when we woke up the next day, the ground was covered in a deep blanket of white. We thought Dad had arranged it. We thought it was a miracle.

I stop at a red light and stand at the very edge of the curb, my tongue stuck out to catch snowflakes. I catch one, the flake cold against my tongue for just a second before it melts. The light turns green and I walk across the street to the alley that shortcuts to home. The alley is a dark tunnel. The garbage bags and cans are capped with snow. In the street at the

very end of the tunnel, a red stoplight blinks. I'm looking at the light when suddenly I see a silver Pontiac
Parisienne zip across the opening like a giant phan-
tom fish.

I know it's my dad.

a slippery silver fish

I run down the alley as fast as I can. I have to catch that silver fish and see for myself who's inside. The ground is slippery, and I slide all the way along the dark tunnel. When I burst onto the street, I can see the car idling at the intersection. I run toward it, yelling at the top of my lungs.

"Hey! Hey! Wait!"

The car starts to pull away just as I reach the corner. I can't make him out, but I'm pretty sure it's Dad. I haven't laid eyes on him in years, but I would recognize him anywhere. There's a blond woman sitting next to him and a small child in the back seat.

They're laughing about something and don't notice me running and yelling after them.

"Hey, wait!" I shout, but the silver fish darts across the street. I make a snowball and whip it at the car. "Come back!" The snowball arcs smoothly, falling just behind the car. I throw another and another, running recklessly into the intersection. A car skids to a stop beside me, the driver cursing as I stumble past.

"Watch where you're going!"

I ignore him and run across the intersection. I can see the boy in the back seat of the Pontiac turned around and staring at me through the window. His face is pale and empty. The Pontiac slips in and out of the lamplight and is gone as quickly as it appeared.

"Come back!" I scream again, even though I know the car is long gone. I fall to the ground and slam my fists in the snow, unaware that the man who almost hit me has been watching the whole time.

"Are you OK, kid?"

I don't answer, but stand up and fix my scarf, then turn and walk back across the intersection. I want to scream at the man to leave me alone and mind his own business. He shakes his head and drives on. My mind is spinning like a Tilt-A-Whirl. What is Dad doing here? Why wasn't he back in the States? Why didn't he come to visit us? I think about him and that woman. I think about them laughing and enjoying themselves like we don't even exist. Does that woman know he has another family? Why was she any better than Ma? And what about the kid? Who was he?

Suddenly I realize that I've lost the brown bag with the little fawn inside.

"Oh, no, no, no!"

I search the street frantically, but I can't see the bag. The snow is falling so heavily now that my own footprints are nearly covered. I start to panic for the little fawn, and run back and forth along the street. How could I have been so stupid? At last I see a small brown pouch at the side of the road in front of the alley. I must have dropped it when I made that first snowball.

When I reach the bag, I see that it has been run over by a car. The top is crushed and dirty. My heart sinks to see that the tiny basket is flattened on one side. The little fawn is fine, however, sleeping peacefully beneath the blanket despite all the commotion. For some reason, the sight of the fawn in its damaged basket makes me feel so sad and sorry for myself that I can't stop the tears from coming.

When I get home, Cid and Queenie are sitting by the fire. They look at me kind of funny, because they wonder where I've been and they can see that I've been crying. I sniff hello and then go straight to my room so they won't ask me anything. I stay upstairs for a long time, trying to decide if I should tell them about Dad or not. I try to fix the basket. The straw is broken and can't be straightened properly. I have no choice but to give it to Cid the way it is. The disappointment sits in my stomach like a rock. I wanted it to be perfect. I wanted it to be better than the ones Dad gave her. I cover the fawn with the little blanket, then tie the tissue around it with a piece of ribbon. It looks small and worthless. As I place the fawn in my drawer, I decide not to tell the girls that I think I saw Dad—yet.

Christmas morning finally arrives. The snow is falling more heavily than ever. The wind has picked up, too, causing big drifts to form on the lawns and streets. The plows have been running all night. The snow is so bad that there are no cars on the road. Normally this kind of weather would make me crazy with excitement, but given the events of the past few days, I can't help feeling a bit numb. I haven't been to the barn in three days, which is really terrible—I've never missed a day before. But I've been feeling so low, it was all I could do just to finish my Christmas shopping.

When I get downstairs, Queenie and Cid are already up, digging through their stockings, which Ma has filled with mittens she knitted at the office, and oranges, and candy canes, and things she found at Woolworth's. The rule in our house is you're allowed to rummage through your stocking first thing Christmas morning—even if you are the only person up—but you have to wait until after breakfast to open your main gifts. I don't know who came up with this rule, but we've stuck to it since I can remember.

"Did you look out the window at the snow?" Queenie asks, as I shuffle into the living room.

"Yeah, I saw it. It's pretty bad out."

"It's worse than bad, Nat. It's crazy. It's supposed to blizzard for days!"

Queenie's enthusiasm is like medicine. I decide to cast off my glum face and make the best of it, as Ma would say. I tuck the little fawn in its tissue wrapping into the branches of the tree and place my gifts for Ma and Queenie beside the few carefully wrapped gifts on the floor. Ma is busy in the kitchen, making pancakes with real maple syrup. Her boss gave her the syrup as a gift, which I think was really considerate of him. Ma lets us eat in the living room by the fire this morning—a special treat for Christmas. I help her carry the plates of pancakes, the small syrup bottle looped through my pinkie.

"Don't take so much syrup, Queenie, or it won't last longer than one meal," Cid scolds.

"It's OK," Ma says. "When it's gone, it's gone. It's Christmas, so let's not be stingy."

I'm with Ma. I've had enough scrimping and scraping for a lifetime. My mind wanders to Dad and the laughing woman, and I can feel the rage spark in my heart again.

"Aren't you going to look in your stocking, Nat?" Queenie asks.

I look through my stocking just to please her, even

though I know it contains exactly the same things as the other stockings.

When we're done with breakfast, Ma lets us open our gifts. Queenie gives everyone cornhusk dolls that she learned to make in art class. Cid gives me a set of red glass clackers. They've been outlawed at school because kids have been fighting with them or clacking them so hard they explode, so I'll have to use them at home. Ma gets bubble bath from Cid and the same thing from me, plus some bars of Pears soap because I know she likes it but won't buy it for herself. I give Queenie the tins of hoof paint— one black and one silver—and a package of Silly Putty. Her face brightens like I just gave her a million dollars. She rushes over and hugs me. She puts the two tins of hoof paint in the pockets of her house robe. The unwrapping continues. Ma gives Queenie a mood ring and a watercolor kit with brushes and palettes and rows of colorful little paints. Cid gets a mood ring, too, a shirt, and a makeup set. I get a Stretch Armstrong from Ma instead of the Luke Skywalker action figure that I wanted. I can't help but feel disappointed, even though I know it's not her fault. The stores have been sold out for months. I open a strange box containing an unfinished sweater sleeve, the needles still tucked in the loops of wool.

"I didn't have time to finish it," Ma sheepishly says as I produce the half-knitted sleeve from the box. "It's going to be nice, though. Look, there's the pattern at the bottom of the box."

I look at the pattern. It shows a young, successful-looking man modeling the sweater, standing with one foot on a rock. In the photo, the sweater is off-white with thick cables that twist down the front. "So this is what a half-knit looks like," I say, just to make Ma laugh.

We play on these words for a while, calling each other half-knits, making up sentences with the expression *half-knit* and such. We do this until we've wrung all we can from the joke and we're all laughing.

"I'm making yours in moss green because I thought it would look nice with your brown eyes," Ma finally explains. "And it will stay clean longer," she adds.

"It'll be really nice, Ma," I tell her, putting the unfinished sleeve back in its box and pushing it under the tree.

Then I give Cid the fawn. She holds the tissue

package in her hand and looks at it for a bit before loosening the ribbon.

"It's not as much as I wanted to give," I tell her apologetically.

Cid unwraps the tissue, revealing the little fawn inside. It's sleeping peacefully, the tiny blanket tucked around its shoulders. Cid looks at me in amazement. "Oh, Nat, it's beautiful!"

"I'm sorry about the basket. It got kind of wrecked. . . ."

"It doesn't matter. The little fawn is beautiful."

She holds it delicately in her hand, showing it to Ma and Queenie.

"It's adorable," Queenie says, admiring the little blanket, then tucking it back around the fawn.

"I was hoping you could start your collection over again," I explain.

Cid carries the fawn up to her room. Queenie and I follow. We watch her place it carefully on top of her dresser.

"I know it won't replace the others right away, but it's a start," I say.

"It's nicer than the ones Dad bought," Queenie says. "He never gave Cid one in a little bed."

Cid fixes the blanket around the fawn. "I love it."

We all stare at the fawn for a while, then go back downstairs to where Ma is cleaning up the living room. We help tidy, but Ma can tell we're anxious to get to the barn to see Smokey.

"Go on," she says. "It'll be a Christmas gift of sorts just to have the house to myself. Mind you bundle up. This weather is getting worse by the minute."

And she's right. You can barely see the big maple tree on our front lawn, the snow is blowing so badly. We're the only ones out in the street. The wind whips at our faces. The snow pelts our clothes and sticks in our eyelashes and hair.

"Only a half-knit goes out in weather like this," I joke.

Cid and Queenie laugh.

"I don't think we'll be riding Smokey outside today. Looks like we'll have to take turns riding him in the barn."

"If we ever make it there," Cid says.

We pull our scarves over our noses and tip our chins into our chests to keep the snow from blinding us altogether. It takes us nearly three times as long to make it up the hill to the end of the lane that leads to the barn. When we get there, the lane is erased by smooth white drifts.

"Doesn't look like anyone's been here," I say.

We cut through the drifts with our bodies, the snow up over our hips in some places. I go first. Then Cid and Queenie. I can feel the carrots that I brought for Smokey in my pants pocket. Despite the cold, I'm sweating from the effort of moving through so much snow. When we reach the barn, we see that the drifts practically cover the door. We start to dig with our hands, clearing a space. We dig and dig until finally we have enough room to open the door a crack. I squeeze inside and push the door with my whole body. The door creaks and groans. I manage to open it enough that Cid and Queenie can come through.

Inside, the horses are wide-eyed and spooked, including Smokey. He's spinning around in his stall, tossing his head and pawing at the ground. The other horses are shifting and snorting. We go into Smokey's stall and calm him with carrots and gentle talk. He responds right away, lowering his head against my stomach as I scratch his ears.

"I don't think anyone else has been here for days," Cid says. "None of the horses have much food."

"Did you top up their bins yesterday?" I ask.

Cid and Queenie exchange nervous looks. Queenie pulls the tins of hoof paint from her coat pockets and places them in the wooden box with the brushes. "We were afraid of Clem," she finally blurts out. "The wind was blowing and the snow was whipping against the windows. We thought we heard voices upstairs."

"Well, it's not our job to watch the other horses," I say, even though we do anyway. For some reason, the people in this barn don't seem to care much about their animals, except maybe for the Gorilla. But even he hadn't come yet today. I can't help but think they're all just a bunch of creeps. "Go get some hay and we'll feed them. We can't let these horses go hungry on Christmas. And who knows when their owners will come, with this storm going on. I imagine some of them are stranded by the weather."

I don't know if this is true, but I'd rather the girls believe that it's the storm and not irresponsibility that's keeping the owners away. This makes us all feel a little bit better about the horses being neglected on Christmas day.

Cid and Queenie busy themselves by throwing

flakes of hay from the loft into the aisle below. When they have enough for all the horses, they climb down the ladder and begin stuffing hay into the feed troughs. The horses nicker hungrily.

"Give them water, too. And don't forget to sprinkle the hay to keep the dust down," I call out from Smokey's stall.

I fill Smokey's trough with hay and top up his water. Then I take the currycomb and start to brush the dirt and dust from his coat. I rub the comb along the roots of his mane, where I know he likes it the most. He closes his eyes contentedly, blowing softly through his nose. The storm rages outside, battering the dirty windows of the barn with snow. I put my arms around Smokey's neck, just to feel the life in him.

I'm holding him like this, my face pressed against his neck, when I hear Cid scream from the back room.

"Nat! Come here!"

"Oh, Nat, hurry!" Queenie cries.

Smokey throws his head back in fright. I run from the stall, slamming the door shut behind me. When I reach the back room, Cid and Queenie are staring into Jed's stall, their hands covering their mouths in horror. I see a huge beam lying across the trough. Beneath the beam lies Jed, his neck all twisted and broken, his legs stiff and sticking out from his body. His eyes are open and his tongue is blue and pinched between his teeth, just like I imagined Clem's would have been. In the background, the radio is faintly playing "Dancing Queen," as though nothing was wrong.

"Oh, my God . . ." It's all I can say, because I can't believe what I'm looking at.

"What happened?" Queenie chokes out. "What happened to him, Nat?"

I know what happened. It's all too clear. The poor horse pushed his head between the rungs of his stall to grab a few wisps of hay that were outside his reach. But getting his head through was easier than getting it back out, and he panicked. All his kicking and slamming around must have loosened that beam and it fell, breaking his neck.

"He must have been starving," Queenie sobs. "It's all our fault. We should have fed him."

"It's not your fault," I tell her. "Ted Henry should have been here taking care of him."

But Queenie is inconsolable. She wails bitterly into her hands.

"What are we going to do?" Cid asks.

"I guess we have to go tell Ted. It's the right thing to do. He'll have to call the disposal."

"But it's Christmas," Cid says. "No one'll be working today. How can we stay here with Jed like that? It's just awful, Nat!"

"We have to go tell Ted," I say soberly. "Christmas or not, he has to do something about it."

We check to make sure that Smokey is OK, then tighten our scarves and make our way through the storm again. I have to push extra hard on the door just to open it. The snow has already erased our tracks. The wind seems worse than ever, tearing at our coats and our hair. We have to yell to hear each other over the roar. We shield our eyes from the snow. It hits our faces like handfuls of dry rice.

It seems to take forever to reach Ted's house. When we get there, Queenie and Cid wait at the bottom of the stairs. I bang loudly on the door several times before it opens. Ted stares at me angrily, like he's been drinking. I don't care because I'm madder than hell. I lay right into him and I don't let him get a word in.

"You better get to the barn, because your horse is dead! A beam fell on him and broke his neck. He was trying to find hay. He's all twisted up in there. You better do something about it right away!"

To my surprise he looks shocked and doesn't say anything. I point right at him and go on.

"You should be ashamed of yourself, neglecting him like that. It's your fault he's dead. If he had food, he wouldn't have stuck his head through the rungs in the first place!"

I don't know if what I'm saying makes any sense to him. He's just staring at me. His stupid mouth is opening and closing like a goldfish's, but nothing's coming out. I turn and stamp down the stairs, leaving him gaping in the doorway. Cid and Queenie loop their arms through mine as we make our way in the snow.

"Can we go home, Nat?" Cid asks. "I can't stand the idea of being there with Jed dead like that."

I nod. I don't like the idea, either. It was bad enough dealing with Clem, let alone the ghost of a mistreated horse. *Well, at least Clem has company now,* I think. I imagine him riding around on Jed like a demon. I imagine them both, half decayed, their bones visible in places. It makes me shiver. I shake my head to get the picture out of my mind.

"Don't tell Ma about Jed," I yell over the roar of

the storm. "She'll never let us go to the barn again if she hears about this."

We lean into the wind, struggling through the storm in silence. The only thing I can hear is the sound of my own breathing through my scarf.

what happens next

Ma wonders what's up when we come back home so soon. I tell her that the weather was so awful, we just tended to Smokey and came home. Ma is happy with this explanation and even commends us on our common sense, which makes me feel bad.

Cid and I spend the rest of the day sitting by the fire. We drink tea, listen to the storm, and talk in whispers about what happened and what we think is going to happen next. Queenie sneaks off to her room to dance. She does it in private so no one will catch her and tell her to stop. I know she is still suffering with guilt over the whole deal, no matter what Cid and I say.

To be honest, I feel responsible as well, consider-
ing why Queenie and Cid had to go to the barn
alone. What if I hadn't been so angry about Cheryl?
I never would've been in the bath, and Cid never
would've kicked the door in. What if I hadn't hidden
Cid's figurines and she hadn't broken them? I wouldn't
have had to take the day to go looking for the fawn.
I would have been at the barn, and Queenie and
Cid wouldn't have been so afraid of Clem's ghost.
We would have checked on all the horses, including
Jed. But a guy can go crazy thinking about all these
what-ifs.

By morning the storm is over, but we take our time
getting ready to go to the barn. We're all dreading
the idea of seeing Jed again. We talk about it the
whole way, trying to ease our fears. We drag our feet,
even though the going is much easier because the day
is clear and quiet, which seems somehow strange
after all that wind.

When we get to the barn, the lane has been plowed.
A truck with a horse trailer is idling in front of the
barn. We exchange nervous glances, then go inside.
The Gorilla is there, packing up his things.

"Damned if I'm going to keep my horse in this barn," he rages. "If it's not people stealing my tack, it's beams falling down. I've had enough!"

I remember the noseband in my coat pocket and feel a rush of guilt. Cid and Queenie don't even know that I still have it. I tried to put it back that night Cheryl and I were here. I never meant to keep it.

Despite our fear, we walk cautiously to the back room. But the only reminder of the horrible event is the fallen beam. It's been pushed to one side, the butt end still resting in the trough where it ended Jed's life. Ted Henry is nowhere in sight.

"You won't find anything to gape at," the Gorilla calls after us. "The sordid deal has been addressed. You kids should get out while you can. The whole damned place could come crashing around your heads."

The Gorilla continues to rant like this as he cleans out his belongings. He sure didn't waste a minute finding another barn to keep his colt, which makes me wonder what he was doing here in the first place. I mean, it definitely wouldn't be my choice if I had a choice at all. But three kids with a free pony and a paper-route income can't be choosers, so to speak.

We sit and watch him as he leads the colt from the

barn and into the trailer. I even help him with the door. When the colt is secure, he starts to back his truck out slowly.

"Wait!" I shout, running up to the truck. I pull the noseband from my coat pocket and hand it to him.

He stares at it, then looks at me.

"I'm sorry," I mumble.

The Gorilla sighs and nods knowingly. "Keep it," he finally says. "And good luck."

I walk back to the barn, the noseband in my pocket, my heart as heavy as a stone. "What about Smokey, Nat?" Queenie asks. "What if more beams fall?"

"They won't," I say, even though I am afraid that they will. "This old barn has been standing for a hundred years and it will stand for a hundred more. That beam fell because Jed got his head stuck like that. It won't happen again."

We all stand there saying nothing, the weight of my words pressing down on us. None of us feels good about the situation. I wish we had a truck with a trailer and somewhere else to go, but we don't.

Back in the barn, Queenie fashions a little cross out of straw and places it on the trough where Jed fell. When she's done, I tie a piece of binder twine across the doorway that leads back to that part of the barn. It isn't much, but somehow it makes us feel better, as though the twine somehow separates us from the horrible event and all it signifies.

We take extra care grooming Smokey. We stop every so often just to look at him and to hug him, which we always do, but today we do it more than ever. The mood is heavy and sad, no matter what we say to change it. We don't talk about what happened to Jed or even mention his name, but our eyes and our faces show how we really feel.

and no birds sing

With all that happened over the holidays, I forgot
about being angry at Cheryl. Now I'm walking to
school and I don't have a clue what to do when I see
her. Maybe I'll ignore her, like she isn't even there. Or
maybe I'll give her a piece of my mind and tell her
what a little witch she really is. Maybe I'll punch
Tyler in the face in front of the whole school and
then walk over and plant a kiss right on Cheryl's
mouth. I'll do that, then walk away and leave her
standing there wishing for more.

But I don't do any of these things. When I get to
history class, she's sitting in her seat. I just sit in

my seat, too, and try to think of a way to turn around and take a look at her, the same as always. When I do manage to catch a glimpse, she doesn't even notice me. She's bent over her book—in her blue sweater and looking prettier than ever—poring over some boring bit of history. Just looking at her, so beautiful like that, I suddenly know that I'm doomed. I'll never be able to say no to her, or be mean to her, or ignore her. I'll never be able to get over her, ever.

It's the same way in English class, only she sits in front of me, so I have no control over the situation. We're studying John Keats, and I finally understand why he wrote "La Belle Dame Sans Merci." I am that "wretched wight" loitering on the cold hillside, and Cheryl is the ruthless faery child, luring me in with her beauty and her enchanting faery song. She stole my heart and made me think she loved me. I even gave her a ride on my horse, just like the man in the poem. And now my soul is damned to wander like the pale and gaping kings and princes and warriors that Keats wrote about, their "starv'd lips" held open in eternal warning. No wonder Keats died at twenty-six. I let out an involuntary moan and look up to find the entire class—including the teacher—looking at me.

"Would you like to share with the rest of the class?" Mr. Schneider asks.

"No, sir."

Mr. Schneider looks at me with curiosity. The rest of the class just stares, all pale and gaping like those damned souls in the poem—except for Cheryl, whose icy blue eyes give me nothing.

The bell rings, and I'm set free to wrestle with my plight. I feel a bump on my shoulder and turn to find Cheryl brushing past me, as though we had never even spoken. Tyler is waiting in his car in front of the school. Cheryl jumps in, and they speed off around the corner. So that's the way it's going to be.

The kids shove past me on the stairs. My heart aches like it's being stomped on by a thousand dirty sneakers. My legs feel weak, and I think I'm going to faint. And now I wish that Cheryl really had never spoken to me. I wish she'd never enchanted me with her beauty and her faery song. I was fine before, when I thought I didn't have a chance, but now I'm lost forever.

• • •

I leave school early and race up the hill to get to the barn. I have to see Smokey. I have to feel his warmth and life against me. Cid and Queenie will catch up to me later, I tell myself as I crunch through the snow up the hill.

That's when I see the silver Pontiac. It drifts right past me and slows to a stop at the top of the hill. I tear up the street and skid alongside the car, pounding my hands on the driver's side window.

"Dad!"

The man turns and looks at me, and I feel as though I've been shot through the stomach. It's not my dad. It's some stranger I've never seen before. He rolls down the window.

"Can I help you, son?"

I shake my head and back away like I've seen a ghost. "I . . . I'm sorry, mister. I thought you were someone else."

I turn and run across the street to the lane that leads to the barn. I feel stupid and embarrassed, but most of all, I feel mad. I know now that Dad will never come back. I guess it's pride or disappointment that makes me decide this next thing, but whatever the reason, I can't help it. I decide not to tell Cid and

Queenie about the Pontiac. I decide that as far as I'm concerned, I don't care if I never see my dad again. As far as I'm concerned, he may as well be dead.

Inside the barn, I discover several empty stalls. In fact, nearly all of them are empty. Pip and the palominos are gone. There are only two horses left, Flag and the quarter horse mare named Silver. Silver will be next to go, I think.

Smokey snorts softly as I walk along the aisles of abandoned stalls. He must know that something is up. I feel sorry for him, not knowing why all the other horses are leaving. I go in Smokey's stall and he leans against me, his gentle eyes blinking in confusion, his head lowered against my stomach.

"It's OK, boy," I tell him.

I rub his mane and speak words of encouragement, but they sound empty, even to me. There's a bang on the door, and Cid and Queenie tumble in from the cold. They see my sad face and look around the empty barn.

"Where'd they all go?" Queenie asks.

"They're gone. Same as the Gorilla. Nobody wants to keep their horse in a barn that's falling down."

Cid looks at me in dismay. "But you said it wasn't

falling down. You said it's been standing for a hundred years and it'll stand for a hundred more."

She says this with concern, not anger, because she wants me to tell her that everything's going to be OK. But I can't. Not today. Not after everything. Not after Dad and Cheryl and Jed and all the empty stalls. It's too much, even for me.

"What does this mean, Nat?" Queenie asks.

"It doesn't mean anything. We're going to stay until we have to leave. Those other people left because they felt guilty. They never took good care of their horses, and they're afraid the same thing will happen to their horses as happened to Jed. They've probably gone off to some stupid, fancy barn where other people feed and ride your horse for you."

Cid and Queenie say nothing. I'm sure they're thinking the same as me about choices and options and whatnot. But we can't all start thinking like that or we're done.

I pull the Gorilla's noseband from my pocket.

"Nat! How could you?" Cid gasps, thinking I'd stolen it.

"It's OK," I tell her. "He gave it to me. He felt sorry for us, I guess."

Cid thinks about this, then nods solemnly.

"Come on," I say at last. "Let's gear Smokey up and take him for a ride around the field."

We spend the next hour taking turns on the sled. Smokey draws us along without a fuss. He doesn't once try to bolt. Even he seems to understand that things will never be the same.

things fall apart

By the time the first green of spring is pushing up through the snow, all the other horses have been moved out. The barn is lonelier than ever now. The sliding doors creak and bang in the wind, but it isn't the same haunted sound as before. It's empty, like the sound of something giving up. I can't even feel Clem hanging around in the rafters anymore.

This makes us uneasy about the future of things, but at least we don't have to worry about sneaking around to get hay and straw for Smokey. There's enough in the loft to last a small pony for years. And we don't even have to pay rent, because Ted Henry is never around. I guess he doesn't feel right taking our money when we're the only ones left. Or maybe he's just ashamed to talk to us after what happened with Jed. Besides, ten dollars a month won't buy him enough of anything to justify the asking.

We tend to Smokey as always, but we're empty of joy. We go through the motions, just waiting for the ax to fall. With every day, the feeling grows that we're running out of time.

I'm sitting in class when an announcement comes over the PA system for me to go to the office. The other kids stare at me as though I'm in the worst kind of trouble, but I can't imagine what I've done. The secretary is waiting for me in the office.

"Your mother phoned. There was a fire at the barn."

She stares at me to see my reaction. My mind goes white. "What do you mean? Where's Smokey? What about my pony?"

"The fire's out, but I don't know anything about your pony. Your mother said to let you out of school early, so you're free to go—if you want to."

She adds this last bit like it would be a bad decision for me to leave. Of course I want to leave early!

What did she think I was going to do? Hang around in class while my pony burns in a fire? I don't even grace her with an explanation. I just turn and run out of the office.

The first thing I think is that I'd better grab Cid. I can't face this by myself. I run across the street as fast as I can. There's a group of no-goods smoking in front of the high school. One of them hollers at me as I run by. I'm afraid of getting lost inside the school because there are several stairways and every one seems to lead to nowhere, but then I see a small sign that says OFFICE, so I run down the hall in that direction.

The secretary at Cid's school is no better than mine, thumbing slowly through a binder looking for Cid's homeroom number like she has all the time in the world. She finally finds what she's looking for, then calls over the PA. Cid appears in the doorway almost immediately. I tell her about the fire and we all but fly out of the office, leaving the secretary just standing there.

We burst out the school doors, running toward the barn. Then suddenly I stop. "What about Queenie? We can't just go without telling her."

"But what if Smokey's dead?" Cid says. "What if he's all—"

She doesn't finish but I know what she's thinking. *What if Smokey's all burned?* I can't let my mind rest on this thought.

"We have to get her. It's only right that we go together."

The principal at Queenie's school doesn't want to let her go, but I convince him he has to. I even tell him to call Ma, which he does, and Ma confirms our story. The next thing we know, we're running full tilt up the hill. With every beat of my shoes on the pavement, I move one step closer to what I'm sure is disaster. I don't want to think such bad thoughts, but my mind won't stop. I see Smokey trapped in his stall, the flames jumping and leaping all around him, his eyes rolling in terror as he tries to kick his way out. I imagine his tail and his mane all singed. I see him jumping over the fence in the field and running off, only to be hit by a car and killed.

I imagine all these things until I feel like I'm going to scream with fear and worry. I think about how the fire started and why. I can't help thinking that Ted Henry himself must have done it, for the insurance or something. I'm all ready to blame him, even though I have no idea if he's responsible or not.

"This is so horrible," Cid keeps saying, over and over.

Queenie runs beside us, her face a picture of worry. I'm sure she'd love to disappear inside her head and dance the whole thing away. But she can't. Not this time.

When we get to the barn, I can see that the roof has collapsed. The smell of burned wood and hay hangs in the air. There are a few gawkers standing around.

"Where's our pony?" I yell at one of the men.

The man looks at me in shock. "He's all right," he finally says. "He's around back in the field. A neighbor saw the fire and let him out. You kids are lucky, all right," he adds. "This could have been a catastrophe. A real catastrophe."

He says this as though it was our fault the barn caught on fire. I guess it must seem strange to him that we're the only ones keeping a horse here in these conditions. I guess he thinks we have choices.

We rush around the barn to the field. Smokey whinnies loudly when he sees us and canters up to the fence. We jump the fence to check him over. He is so happy to see us, he places a hoof on my shoe in greeting.

"He's fine. He's OK," I tell Cid and Queenie, who go over him, looking for scratches and bruises. "Aside from being really lonely, I think he's none the worse for the situation."

But none of us wants to leave. We stay until it grows really dark. Before we go, we fill a bucket with water and place it in the field with Smokey. I check the latch on the gate to make sure it's secure.

"What are we going to do now, Nat?" Queenie asks.

"He'll be fine here until we can think of something. There's enough grass coming up to keep him fed, and now that it's warmer, he should be OK staying outside overnight."

"What about all our stuff—Smokey's sign and our brushes? Do you think they were burned in the fire? And what about the sled?"

I was thinking all these things, too, and I didn't have an answer. "Well, we can't go in just yet. We'll wait until things die down so we can sneak in and get our things. But we'll have to wait until tomorrow or maybe even later, when no one's around."

Ma is waiting for us when we get home. Her face looks old and drawn.

"Is Smokey all right? The man who called couldn't tell me much."

We tell her all about the fire and what we think happened. We tell her about Smokey being fine out in the field. Ma listens intently. She doesn't ask many questions, but lets us tell the story without interruption. When we're finished, she leans back in her chair and lets out a heavy sigh. She looks at us long and hard, and I can tell she's ready to drop a bomb.

"There's no easy way to say this. We have to sell the house."

"What?!"

"We have to sell the house. We have no choice. I can't keep up with it."

Cid and I howl in protest. Queenie slips into the living room and starts to dance.

"You can't sell the house, Ma! Where are we going to live?"

"There's an apartment up the street for rent. It's big enough for all of us."

"What if we don't want to live in an apartment? What if we don't want to go?"

"Nathaniel, we have no choice," Ma says with resignation.

"But I can help you, Ma. I can help pay the bills."

Ma stares at me, her shoulders rounded and her eyes sad. "I know you would, Nat. I know. But the money you earn from your paper route isn't enough to dig us out of the hole we're in. We have no choice but to sell. I wasn't going to tell you just yet, with the fire at the barn and all. . . ."

"Sounds like you've already made up your mind."

Ma looks at the floor. "I have. A man came around today saying he has a buyer. All I have to do is sign the offer."

"How much are they going to pay?" I ask with disdain.

"It's a good offer, Nat. It's more than we paid for the place."

"So that's it?" Cid shouts. "That's all there is to it? We just leave and never see our house again? And then what? We just keep moving and moving forever? Why don't you just shoot us all in the head?!"

Ma's voice disappears to a whisper. "My hands are tied."

Cid and I leave the table in disgust. I feel bad leaving

Ma like that. I can tell she is tired and broken. I can tell she can't go on struggling anymore. But I can't help myself. I don't know how much more I can take. I thought the barn catching on fire was bad, but this is worse.

Ted Henry is waiting for us when we get to the barn the next day. "You kids have to move your pony out. He can't stay here. It ain't safe."

I just stare at him with hatred. Somehow I'm sure this is all his fault.

"Where are you going to take him?" he asks.

"I'm not sure yet, but we'll find a place."

"Well, I know someone who wants to buy him, if you're interested."

Cid and Queenie look at me in horror. We never even considered that we'd have to get rid of Smokey.

"Well, we're not selling," I say angrily.

Ted shrugs. "Suit yourself. I just thought I'd let you know. It's a good home that wants him. A young boy over in Bolton. He wants to jump him in the pony club."

We spend the night at home combing through the want ads in the paper. There are stalls for rent, but they are either too far away or too expensive. We talk in circles for hours, trying to come up with a solution. By the end of the night, selling Smokey seems to be the only thing we can do. Now I understand Ma's decision about the house. I feel ashamed for the way I treated her.

Cid sits on the edge of the bed sniffling quietly. Queenie dances off to one side, lost in her secret world. I wish I could dance or just sit on the bed and cry, but I know it won't change anything. I know what we have to do.

a terrible decision

The next day I find myself standing on Ted Henry's porch again, banging on his door. He whips the door open as usual, but this time he doesn't seem angry.

"Come to your senses?" he asks.

"How much are they willing to pay?"

"One hundred and fifty dollars."

"Is it a good home? Do you know the people?"

"I know them enough. They're rich. They've got a big barn and riding arenas and the whole bit. They'll take good care of him, if that's what you're worried about."

I am worried about that, and a million other things, too. Like, will they love him, and comfort him when he's lonely or scared? Will they give him carrots for treats, and wet his hay to keep the dust down? Will they rub his mane the way he likes? I can feel a big lump growing in my throat.

"Tell them OK," I say at last. "Tell them we'll sell."

Ted nods, like we've made the best decision.

I drag myself down the stairs to where Queenie and Cid are waiting. I can't look into their eyes or I know I'll break down. Somebody has to be strong, and I know it has to be me.

"This is it, isn't it?" Cid says.

I can't even bring myself to answer her. Queenie reaches out for my hand, and we walk back to the barn. When we reach the lane, there is no one else there. Queenie and Cid go around to the field while I sneak inside to recover our things. The inside of the barn is littered with boards. Light from outside filters in through the holes in the roof, but the barn is still somehow dark. Beneath the loft, the ladder lies in a heap, collapsed in the heat of the fire. The windows are smashed where the firemen broke through with their hoses, and the smell of smoke is so thick, it chokes me. Smokey's stall looks small and dark without him in it.

I pick through the rubble over to where we keep our tack. I grab the brushes and hoof-picks and roll them up in Smokey's blanket. I grab the twine harness and the sled. It's warped slightly from the heat. I grab Queenie's bridle and loop it over one shoulder, and then I grab the sign and the Gorilla's noseband. When I have everything, I stop to take a good, hard look around.

"This really is it," I say to myself, echoing Cid's words. I think of all the life that has gone on here. I think of all the animals and people that have come through these doors and walked along these aisles. And now they're gone. Gone forever. There is nothing worth saving. No life left. No horses, no people, no ghosts—nothing.

Ted Henry doesn't waste any time arranging the sale. We're set to meet the people after school the next day. As usual, I suspect Ted and wonder what he's getting out of it. He's probably charging the people twice as much money as he told us and keeping half for himself. I fuel my anger for a while thinking about this.

That night we sit on my bed talking about what will happen. Cid is trying to think of some way to prevent the inevitable. She suggests running away with Smokey. She wants to travel from town to town, riding Smokey and camping out. She even thinks about getting a rifle for protection. I don't mind the idea, but we both know it won't work.

With all our talking, we don't notice that Queenie is nowhere in sight. We check her room to see if she's gone to bed, but she's not there. We check through the whole house, careful not to alert Ma.

"Where is she?" Cid asks.

"I bet she's at the barn!"

Cid and I sneak out of the house so Ma won't hear us and wonder what's going on. We run the whole way, worried that Queenie may be in trouble. When we reach the barn, I can see Smokey in the distance. We climb the fence and make our way through the field, tripping over stones and tufts of grass.

"Queenie!" I call out.

Smokey whinnies. When we get closer, we find Queenie sitting on the ground, her arms wrapped around her knees, the bottles of hoof paint at her feet. Smokey's hooves shine black in the dark, his one white hoof sparkling silver. "Looks really nice," I say.

Queenie sniffles. I sit down next to her and put my arms around her.

"It isn't fair," she says. "It just isn't fair. Why can't things be different for us? Why does everything have to spoil?"

I can't find the words to explain it to her. I can't think of one thing to say to make her feel better. So I just sit there, holding her and staring off into the night. Cid stands next to Smokey, running her fingers through his mane. I wish we could stay in this field forever. I wish things were different for us, too—that we weren't poor and that we had options. I wish I could wave my hand and make everything better.

I pull Queenie close to me. She leans her head on my chest. "I'll ask Ma if we can take school off tomorrow," I say. "I'll explain everything to her. She'll let us do it when she knows why."

Queenie nestles into my arms, and we sit like this for a long time. Then we gather up the hoof paint and make our way home.

Ma doesn't even flinch when I ask her for the day off school. I start to give her some lame excuse, because I don't want to tell her that we've decided to sell Smokey. But she doesn't need an explanation. She says we can take the day and she'll write us notes, too. Before I leave her room, she hands me a box. It's the sleeve that she gave me at Christmas, only now it's a whole sweater. I try it on right there, just to show Ma that I like it and that there are no hard feelings.

"Keep your knits about you," she says in a sad little voice.

how it all ends

Cid, Queenie, and I arrive at the barn early the next morning. Smokey canters down from the top of the field when he sees us. I feed him carrots through the fence before climbing over and putting on his bridle. I hand the reins to Cid, because I know she'll want to ride first. Cid looks at me, then hands the reins to Queenie.

"You go first," she says.

Queenie hops up on Smokey's back without any help. She reins him to the right, then canters over to the fence at the far end of the field. She veers to the left, dipping behind the little hill, then canters to the spot where the giant maple tree grows. She reins

Smokey in and stands beneath the tree for a while, stroking his neck. Smokey chomps on the bit, anxious to go. Queenie spurs him forward and they take off again, Queenie's hair flowing as wildly as Smokey's mane and tail.

Then Cid goes for a ride, following Queenie's path along the fence and to the maple tree. She canters across the field and pulls Smokey to a stop in front of me. She jumps to the ground and hands me the reins. I run my hand along Smokey's neck, rubbing his mane the way he likes before I get on.

I rein him to the right, just like Cid and Queenie did, but I don't let him canter. I walk him to the fence, feeling his muscles move beneath me. He snorts and tosses his head, anticipating the gallop. I keep him close, trotting him easily along the fence to the maple tree. I stop, just the way Cid and Queenie did, then let my legs hang loose at Smokey's sides. The sunlight dances with the leaves of the maple, dappling us with quick patches of light. It's cool beneath the tree; the smell of new grass is in the air. Smokey paws restlessly at the ground. He turns to look at me. I pat him until I'm ready—and then I give him a kick.

We are off, galloping faster than we have ever

galloped before. I shout encouragement in his ears, urging him on. He stretches out his neck, his mane whipping every which way. His breaths are short and hard, and I can feel the power of his muscles and his lungs as he runs. Queenie and Cid are hooting and hollering. They're egging us on, pushing us faster and faster across the field. My heart races, the beats keeping rhythm with the thunder of Smokey's hooves against the ground.

"Go around again!" Cid and Queenie shout as we arc past them.

I rein Smokey around and we continue to gallop until we reach the giant maple tree again. Here I slow him to a walk and let him catch his breath, his sides moving in and out like a bellows. I make him walk nice and slow back across the field. By the time we reach the girls, Smokey is calm and so am I. I don't dismount right away but stay seated, feeling Smokey's warmth.

From where I'm sitting, I'm the first to see the truck. It trundles up the lane, hauling a small trailer behind. It stops in front of the corral, and a boy jumps from the passenger's side, then saunters up to the fence. He looks spoiled and aloof. A man emerges from the driver's side. His shirt and pants are perfectly pressed like he's some model from the Sears catalog. He waves at us, but I just sit there staring. I can't bring myself to wave back like everything's OK. The man opens the latch to the gate and starts walking toward me.

I can't really explain what happens next, but suddenly I just can't go through with the whole thing. Maybe all Cid's talk about running away planted the seed in my mind, I don't know, but before the man reaches me, I rein Smokey around and kick him hard. Cid and Queenie look totally shocked as Smokey bolts straight to a gallop. We tear down the field, me hollering like some crazy cowboy, the sound of Smokey's hooves beating like a war drum.

"Hee-ya! Get up! Go on, get up!"

The fence grows bigger and bigger at the bottom of the hill and I know Smokey can't make it over—not with me on his back. Then I remember the part off to the right, bent low from years of kids cutting across the field. I rein Smokey toward the dip and grab hold of his mane with one hand. He approaches the fence with quick choppy steps, and I think he's going to shy, but then he jumps into the air with a grunt.

To my surprise we clear the fence easily, hitting the ground on the other side with a thud. I slide to one side then regain my seat. Smokey's hooves slip in the spring mud, but he doesn't slow down. I kick him again and urge him forward, the mud splattering against our legs and faces. I feel reckless and wild, like nothing can stop me, like Luke Skywalker when he destroyed the Death Star. For some reason I can't help thinking that this must have been how Dad felt, too, the day he sped away in his silver Pontiac Parisienne. No questions. No explanations. Just the wind in his face and a senseless drive to be free, no matter what the consequences. Maybe running away was all he could think about doing at the time. Maybe he felt he had no choice. Suddenly I feel as though I understand him.

Smokey and I cut down through the park and back out the other side. We keep going full out until we reach the woods on the far end of town. I think I'm pretty safe here, so I slow Smokey to a walk. We move along the path through the trees, Smokey snorting and tossing his head. The sunlight glitters through the branches and leaves. The woods are quiet, save for the sounds of a few birds.

As we walk along, I start thinking. I'm not sure how smart it was to just take off, but I don't care. I feel kind of bad for leaving Queenie and Cid like that, but there was no time to hang around and explain myself. I didn't even know what I was going to do until I did it. Now I have to think of a plan.

Smokey grunts and snorts again contentedly. He's happy to be walking in the woods on such a nice day. I pat his neck firmly. His coat is wet and foaming from the run. "You're a good boy, Smokey."

I think about how furious Ted Henry's going to be when he finds out. Serves him right. It's his fault this whole thing happened anyway. If he were a better person, the barn never would have caught fire in the first place. I bet he'll call the cops on me, though. This gets me worrying. Can they charge someone for deciding not to sell something? I didn't sign any papers. Still, if someone can think of a way to get somebody, it's Ted.

Smokey and I walk until the woods open out into a wide meadow. The sun is warm and inviting. I dismount and tie the reins to a low branch on a nearby tree, then stretch out on the grass to think. I lie like this and let my mind wander. Maybe it's the seriousness of the situation, or the warmth of the sun on my face, but I can't seem to form a plan. Images run through my head of Ted calling the cops, Ma crying, the cops coming to get me, and me growing a beard and living off the land. After several hours of this, I start to feel hungry. Smokey is grazing lazily on the grass at his feet, completely unaware that we are fugitives. He looks magical in the sunlight, like a pony from a fairy tale. I feel scared and unsure of what to do next, but decide that no matter what happens, I'm glad I ran away. A pony like Smokey is worth fighting for—even if we did get him for free. A pony like Smokey is no small thing.

I don't have any food or money with me, so I lean against a boulder in the grass until the sun creeps down from the sky and the meadow turns from green to gold and then gray. The air has grown colder and my hunger pains are getting worse. I'm thirsty, too. I bet Smokey is even thirstier than I am. I decide to wait until it's dark enough to safely venture out of the woods, then take my chances and ride Smokey home, get some money, a few blankets, and some warmer clothes, and take off again—to where, I don't know. I'm hoping an idea will pop into my head along the way.

We pick our way through the forest. The trees are dark and mean-looking in the night. They seem to lean toward us as we move along the path. The branches creak like old coffin lids and the leaves whisper like voices all around us. And there are other strange noises that I can't make out, coming from deep in the woods. I think I hear an owl hoot somewhere in the distance. Scenes from *Night of the Living Dead* keep flashing through my head. Smokey must be scared, too, because he's walking quickly, his ears all pricked up and his eyes wide and searching. I grab a handful of mane, just in case. I hum a tuneless song softly to myself, to take my mind off the situation.

At last we hit the street. I look up and down the road, although I don't know what I'm expecting to see. In any case, it's all clear. I cluck my tongue, urging Smokey on. That's when I notice a police cruiser driving slowly up the hill. I kick Smokey and trot across the road, then duck behind a group of bushes. The cruiser glides past, so close I can see the officer's face illuminated by the dashboard lights. I don't know if Ted called the cops, but I figure it's better to be safe than sorry. Smokey stamps impatiently. I hold the reins in a bit tighter.

When the cruiser is out of sight, we move back onto the street. It's quiet and dark, so I kick Smokey into a canter. We reach the next intersection and run right into the cruiser, coming from the opposite direction. I rein Smokey around in an instant, but it's too late. The cop spots me and gives a quick blast on his siren. So Ted Henry did call the cops! I cut across several lawns and into the backyard of a house. The siren wails and the lights flash as the cruiser streaks around the corner, trying to cut me off. Smokey weaves like a barrel pony, past an old swing set and a rusty barbecue, around a forgotten tricycle and over some garden hose. We burst through the bushes at the back of the house and crash onto the street, just ahead of the cruiser. A branch catches my arm and rips my sleeve. I can hear tires on asphalt, and I don't even have to look back to know the cop is right behind me.

All I can think about is going home. I have to get home. I rein Smokey around and gallop straight into town. The siren grows fainter as we leave the cruiser behind, the cop struggling to turn the car around in the narrow street. Everyone stares open-mouthed as I gallop by—people in shops and in cars and strolling along the street. I nearly hit an old lady who steps out of a store to rubberneck. She dashes back inside as I blast past.

Someone shouts at me. The siren grows louder again as the cruiser speeds along the main street. Just ahead, a set of granite stairs yawns down to the town square. Smokey shies and tries to turn away, but I kick him on. We clatter down the stairs, Smokey's hooves skidding as we hit the pavement at the bottom. The stairs throw the cop for a loop, and we manage to make it all the way to the park before he figures out where we've gone.

As we gallop toward the house, I can feel the cruiser getting closer. My mind races. What are we going to do when we get caught? I imagine myself in jail and Ma crying. I can see the house. The lights are all blazing. We tear up the walk and right to the front steps. I jump from Smokey just as the cruiser screeches up to the house, lights throbbing angrily.

"Joy ride's over, son!"

I freeze, standing at the top of the stairs, reins in one hand, the cruiser lights reflecting like flames against the windows of the house. Some neighbors poke their nosy heads out to see what's going on.

The cop gets out and walks toward me, hitching up his pants at the waist. "What were you running for, son?"

I shrug. Smokey snorts and shakes his head.

"Am I in trouble?"

"You had your mother pretty scared."

Just then, Cid and Queenie burst through the front door. "Nat!" They stare at the cop in amazement.

"Are they going to arrest you?" Queenie asks.

The cop clicks his pen and makes a note in a small book that he pulls from his pocket.

Then Queenie and Cid both start talking at once.

"Where were you?"

"We thought you ran away for good!"

"We were worried sick. Ma called the police and everything."

"You should have seen how shocked that man and his boy were when you took off on Smokey!"

"Everything's OK now, Nat," Queenie says. "Ma said we can keep Smokey. We can use the money from the house!"

Then Ma rushes out the door. She looks as though she's been crying for hours. To my surprise, she doesn't yell, but throws her arms around me, kissing my head and face all over.

"Is this your son, ma'am?" the officer asks.

Ma just stands there, holding me so close I can feel her heart beating in her chest. "Yes, yes, it is."

The officer writes a few more notes, then radios someone at the station. He turns back to me. "You should tell people where you're going next time, you hear?"

"Yes, sir," I mumble.

And then the cop gets in the cruiser, turns off the lights, and drives off. He doesn't even hang around to grill me or anything. I guess that's the advantage of living in a small town. People know when to leave well enough alone.

"Why didn't you tell me, Nat?" Ma finally says when the cruiser is out of sight. "Why didn't you let me know what was going on?"

I can feel a big lump forming in my throat. My head is dizzy and light from lack of food and from riding so hard. "I promised not to worry you about things, Ma."

Ma holds me even tighter. Her body shudders against mine as she cries.

I hold her for the longest time. I don't care who sees us. "Is it true about Smokey, Ma?" I ask at last. "Can we keep him?"

Ma nods and sniffles. She forces a smile. "Come inside, Nat," she says.

Ma runs me a hot bath and makes me a cup of tea, while Cid and Queenie tend to Smokey. They clear out the shed in the backyard to keep him there for the night, just like Queenie had wanted to do from the very beginning. As the hot water pours into the tub, Ma tells me how we can afford to keep Smokey with the money we'll have once we sell the house. She says we'll find some place really nice to keep him. She tells me not to worry about Ted Henry, or the man and his boy who came to buy the pony. She tells me she took care of it and that none of it matters anyway.

When Ma's finished explaining things, I go into the bathroom and close the door. I strip off my dirty clothes and lower myself by inches into the steaming bath. The hot water soothes my tired bones, and despite how hungry I am, I drift off, my mug of tea growing cold on the edge of the tub. The sound of Queenie and Cid fussing around in the backyard filters in through the steam. I can hear Ma, too, the faint clatter of pots being washed in the kitchen. I let myself relax completely, and my mind starts to wander.

I think about the future and what life holds for us. I think about selling the house and where that'll take us. I think about Ma and Queenie and Cid, and all the things we've been through together, and how I never could have survived any of it alone. I think about

Dad and how he's a part of me, whether I like it or not, and Cheryl and Tyler and how I'll never be like either of them.

And then I think way into the future, beyond heartache and the lack of choices. I imagine a place where life is better for us. A place where Queenie won't have to escape inside her dance. A place where Cid isn't angry anymore, and where Ma is happy and secure. And then I go beyond even that, to the whole great world of things, the stars up in the heavens, and the moon, too, its frozen face pale and gaping. I imagine the planets moving silently in their orbits, and the earth tilting on its axis in the inky black of space. And then I imagine Smokey, at the center of it all, cantering in smooth, hypnotic circles, his mane and tail streaming, his hooves thundering tirelessly against the grass.

acknowledgments

Thanks to my family, for everything. Thanks to my editor, Lynne Missen, for her expertise and understanding, and to the entire crew at Harper-Collins Canada. Thanks to my editor at Candlewick, Deborah Wayshak. Special thanks to Ruth Hanley for her endless enthusiasm and support, and to Chris and Richard for pottery and prints and a place to call home.